CODE FOR THE ROAD

TULSA

ISBN: 978-1-957262-92-5
Code for the Road

Copyright © 2023 by Craig Leavitt
All rights reserved.

No part of this publication may be reproduced, distributed, or transmitted in any form or by any means, including photocopying, recording, or other electronic or mechanical methods, without the prior written permission of the publisher, except in the case of brief quotations embodied in critical reviews and certain other noncommercial uses permitted by copyright law.

For permission requests, write to the publisher at the address below.

Yorkshire Publishing
1425 E 41st Pl
Tulsa, OK 74105
www.YorkshirePublishing.com
918.394.2665

Published in the USA

CODE FOR THE ROAD

CRAIG LEAVITT

NOTE TO READERS

The writing of Code for the Road was a more daunting task than I could have ever imagined. It has given me a newfound respect for anyone that has been able to put thoughts together and created a story from them. Thank you to Yorkshire Publishing for helping me to do that.

During the writing of this book, there had been many exciting starts and a lot of frustrating stoppages. But the one constant through all the highs and lows was my wonderful wife, Ann, to whom this book is dedicated. I finally don't have to hear, "Are you working on your book?" anymore…until the next book. I would like to acknowledge Alan Losure. Alan is a neighbor, customer, and friend whose polite coaxing by asking me about how my book was coming, helped pull my attention back to the adventure.

There are a couple real life stories intertwined into the main story. They were told to me by customers as they sat in my barber shop. I "twisted" them around a little bit to fit the narrative of the story. (Can you guess which two?)

I killed them.

I killed both of them.

Both of my parents.

I killed them in many ways.

Any way the story needed to be told, that was the way they had to die. Whatever way it was for me to get away. Whether it was to convince a few men that I was just as dangerous as them or it was to win over an old maid who needed a tad bit more convincing to give me a little more food. When you're hungry, or in my situation, incredibly famished you'd say or do anything to get food.

My parents were loathsome people. Whatever they needed to say or do to get what they believed they needed . . . they did it. Interesting that I just said that. Didn't I just say the exact same thing about myself in the prior paragraph? The difference is that they didn't necessarily NEED to be so heinous to stay alive. It was a choice. Sort of . . . an easy, indecent way to exist. Me? It was my way to survive. Or at least I was afraid it would be.

Catherine and Francis Byrne were my parents. I was an only child of these very unpleasant people. My father was a raging alcoholic with a taste for the cards . . . Or was it that he was a raging gambler with a taste for the drink. Doesn't really matter. My mother was a harlot. Simply put. That's what she was. I wasn't sure if they were like that before they knew each other or if being married brought the worse out of them. I guess it didn't really matter. They were who they were. Their screaming and fighting, begging and pleading with each other was too much to handle. And when the comings and goings of the daily degenerates were added to the mix, then it was more than I could take. I always wondered what it would take for me to get away. What would be my breaking point? Would I even have the courage to leave? I soon realized that I had to leave, or I would become one of them.

Boston in 1887 was a turbulent time. The city's population was growing at an enormous rate from immigrants of at least a dozen countries. The different languages being spoken along with different ways of life made it hard to get along with one another. The immigrants that were here were transported by rail or barges from New York. Most stayed in Boston, but a lot of the newcomers railed on further west. Finding living quarters was hard. People were stacked on top of each other in these dilapidated buildings.

Our living quarters were a great locality for some of the immigrants. Mother used this to her advantage. We were just a few blocks from the rails going west. The shipyards were a little farther due east. Mom said we needed the extra money because of Dad's sinful weaknesses. She would board out my room to anyone looking for any type of railroad employment or to any new immigrants fresh off the boat from whatever homeland they were leaving.

My job as a 12-year-old girl was to come home from school and clean up after the boarders that frequented our residence. These men were pigs. Absolute boars. I could literally hear them snorting and grunting into the wee hours of the night. This was when I realized why boarding in our home was so in demand. My mother was earning extra money by providing comfort and companionship to these swine. Any of them. All of them.

I laid on the living room floor by the window wishing that it would open and let me get some air. The noise of the streets helped drown out most of the noise that came from my room. At least the closed window wouldn't let in the vile smell of rotting trash that had been setting on the curb all week. The influx of people moving into this town so quickly had brought a problem of trash removal. The trash haulers simply could not keep up. Or maybe they're just not concerned about completing their duties since they hadn't been paid in over five weeks. At least that's the word that came from Conor. Conor is the cop that's on the beat in our little slice of heaven. The trash haulers, policemen, and firemen were all talking about striking like they did a few years ago if the local politicians didn't pony up something soon. The "elected" officials sure hadn't missed any meals or a night's sleep while the good ole people of our borough worked tirelessly to perform their duties so they were able to provide all the necessities for their families. Yes, including my profane mother. Blech!

Father. Not Dad. My father was rarely home. Good ole Father Francis was always out looking for the next big win or the next big sucker. As long as the next big win or sucker was produced from bourbon or the racehorses. It seemed there was always someone shouting expletives up to our apartment windows. He was always robbing Peter to pay Paul. But he was a likable guy. I guess that was part of his gimmick. He was so believable he could sway people to spend their money, but he rarely paid them back. He would pay back just enough to the person to keep them from nagging. My father Francis really took advantage of the new immigrants coming in off the ships. He would promise them a quick payday tomorrow for a small payment today. Our ramshackle building was full of those marks and just about everyone that stayed in our place was too.

I presumed he was also somewhat of a gal-sneaker on account of the cheap perfume sprayed over yesterday's cheap perfume that emitted from his soiled shirt collar. I bet his shirt was just as soiled as his latest floozy. I can't imagine that he'd turn down any type of salacious offer. Some nights he wouldn't come home at all. I just sighed and was sure he was in a gutter or a back alley sleeping off the remnants of his escapades. There also were times when those nights turned into weeks where I believed he was in the pokey or what one of mom's "regular renters" liked to call it, the "gray bar hotel." That renter was a Russian immigrant named Nikita. Brute of a man. He was THE symbol of Mother Russia. The Russian Bear.

Now if HE was my father, I believe he'd be my protector from my parents' enemies, and I would have nothing to fear. But he wasn't. And I did have something to fear. I'm not exactly sure how tall he was, but I do know that he had to duck his head when he came through the doorway. I've never seen any man do that. Though he was agile, he also carried enough weight that when he walked through the room the floorboards creaked into submission. I'm sure his long oily hair and tangled beard were populated with lice and food crumbs. He was also one of my father's easiest marks, maybe that was because Nikita was always here "renting" my room. Nikita stumbled from my bedroom picking at his unkempt beard as if he was searching for remnants of his last meal of garlic and boiled beef.

Out the front door of our apartment he went so he could use the community bathroom at the near end of the hall.

The sun had finally gone down for the day but the humidity in this kindling bucket of a building was going up. Mother Catherine stood in the doorway of my bedroom and stared intently at me as I laid on the floor near the window. As she blew smoke from her homemade coffin nail, she slurred in that alcohol-soaked voice of hers, "Don't judge me, Elizabeth. I see you laying there looking down on me. You are no better than me and it won't be long until you'll come to the realization that your life is, and will be, just like mine."

"Don't ever count on me to be like you, Catherine."

"Mom! It is Mom! Do not call me by my name. Show me some respect," interrupted Catherine as I stayed curled up on the threadbare edge of the rug near the window.

"Respect?? The kind of respect that . . . that you show me by having me sleep on this ratty old rug in the living room while you entertain your men??"

"Boarders. They are boarders," she said quietly, wishing it was silent enough so that she couldn't hear her own words. That way, her dirty actions never happened.

This interaction between my mom and me was not out of the ordinary. But as the summer heat rose, so did the volume of our arguments. They would win a gold medal if it ever became an Olympic event.

The early moonlight began to shine through one of the two dirty windows in the living area of our home. The moonlight enhanced the aura of dust surrounding mom as she slowly turned and retreated into the darkness of my room. I just couldn't let her step away from our argument without giving more of my two cents worth. I don't know what caused my angst tonight. Whether it's the sour smell coming in the window from the trash or the trashy smell coming from my room that my mom was sauntering back to. How could I live like this? I had had enough with how my life was going. I could not let this be my future. As the frustration mounted from deep in my being, I simply couldn't hold back much longer. I shouted, "It seems to me that since you have nothing left to say to me and decided to walk away, then I win! Again! You are a loser! Again!"

As fast as lightning, Mom swept back into the room. I must say that I was quite impressed with her agility under her condition. She was about to swing a harsh slap to the side of my head, but it was interrupted when we heard an awful cry coming from someone from the dank hallway. Then a hellacious sound. It sounded like the walls on the other side of the hallway were falling down onto the lower apartment. I had to admit that I had been waiting for the day when this decrepit building would cave in. We rushed to the door. Just when Mom and I reached it, it crashed open as it slammed against the wall barely missing us.

"VERE ES FRANCEES?!" Screamed Nikita in broken English. "I KNOW I SAW HEEM! I SAW HEEM TREW DE CRACK OF DE TUALET (toilet) DOOR! I VANT MY PART OF DE VINNINGS OF LAST RACE! I VANT ALL MY VINNINGS!!"

"MY GOD, HE IS NOT HERE!!" Mom screamed back at him utterly taken by the way this bear had stormed into our space.

Nikita was just inside the doorway, but his presence filled up the entire room. "He, he, he is never here. He's always g-g-gone," she stammered at the sight of this behemoth. For some reason, Nikita looked much larger than before.

"NO! NO! NO! NO! NO! I SAW HEEM. I SAW HEEM VIT MY OWN EYES!" he spat out as a louse scurried back into his beard for protection.

Surely Francis didn't sneak into our apartment when Mom and I were arguing. Dad is a wily sneak. But there was no way he snuck in here during our argument. Just as Nikita finished his tirade, I heard dogs barking outside as if they were spooked. I jumped away from the door and ran over to the grimy window just in time to see a shadowy rail-thin figure haphazardly dropping from the fire escape that was hanging on the opposite end of our building. Surely that wasn't Francis, but it sure looked like him from this far. "Francis!!!!" Someone else shouted. "You owe me money!!!!" It was said from a vague person coming from where the indistinguishable figure landed on the ground. Nikita was not having hallucinations. He was right. He did see him. Francis must have run down the crowded hallway, side-stepping bagged trash that was collecting at its edges just as Nikita had flung open the community bathroom door. I had to admit, I was kind of spellbound with the figure of dad. It seemed like forever since his presence was around here.

"He's not here, Nikita! He's not . . . AAAACCHHHH . . . "

I'm snapped back to the present situation when I heard Mom's sentence trail off to an awful sound.

Nikita was absolutely going berserk. He was choking Mom! He was choking my mom! He had lifted her off her toes by a few feet. Shaking her like one of my rag dolls from my younger days. He was going to kill her if he hadn't done so already. People were standing in the doorway to get a view of the spectacle that was going on in the room as more people from the hallway were cramming their heads in to see what was going on.

"FRANCEES VEEL NO LONGER OWE ME FOR VINNINGS," bellowed Nikita. "HE TOOK ME MONEY FOR DE LAST TIME! HE TOOK MUCH FROM ME! NOW I TAKE FROM HEEM. IT ES TIME FOR ME TO DO, VUT EES WORD . . . YES, YES 'PAYBACK!'" Spittle was coming from his tooth-rotted mouth. Spraying all over my mom. Her rumpled blonde hair lifelessly hung off her head. One thin floral strap of her nightgown hung from her right shoulder. It seemed as lifeless as her. I rushed at him with all the fight in me I could muster. But he swiped me away like one of the flies buzzing around the hallway with his left hand as his right hand kept shaking my mom. His back-handed slap propelled me over the arm of our second-hand couch. Instantly my right ear was ringing, and I could feel my heartbeat above my right eye as it swelled.

It felt surreal. For the first time in a long time, I longed for my mom. Not Catherine this time, but Mom. Nikita tossed her body towards a scuffed-up desk Francis had pilfered from a trash heap somewhere. She skidded over it, spilling dime store china all over the floor. If she wasn't dead from his shaking, she definitely was from her landing. She looked like a marionette that was tossed into a corner with broken limbs pointing in different directions.

"VERE ES THE DEVUSHKA?!" Nikita howled. "FFFRANCEEEE'S GIRL! SHE COME TO ME VIT FISTS. NOW I NEED TO SHOW HER PUNISHMENT! I VILL TREAT HER LIKE I TREAT TRASHED MATB (mother)." Nikita surveyed the shambled room for me, never taking a step away from the spot from where he had tossed mom's body. As he looked for me, I noticed the evil that covered his face as he scanned the room. There was nothing good coming to me from him. Oh no, no, no! I have to get out right now! But there is no way I can get past him and through the door with all the busybodies craning their necks for a view.

"How in the heck do you think you're going to get away with all this wickedness lo uomo (man)?" said our neighbor Mr. Fortunato Gavazzi. He had just recently gotten off a ship from Italy and had picked up English rather fast. He had quickly become known in the tenement as the know-it-all neighbor. He knew everyone's business. If you needed something, he knew who had it. Everyone respected the little old man despite his nosiness. But Nikita was not everyone. Nikita didn't know Mr. Gavazzi nor cared anything about the little bald man. Nikita turned around slowly to the door to decipher which bobble head spoke the words. There was pure fear on everyone's face except for the little old man's. I don't know if Mr. Gavazzi was incredibly fearless or just plain mad as a hatter. Or was he buying me time to figure out an escape? Whatever the case may be, it bought me a few seconds because Nikita pummeled Mr. Gavazzi with two quick jabs to the face. The first one blew up Mr. Gavazzi's nose and the second one seemed to embed Mr. Gavazzi's wire rimmed spectacles into the skin around his eyes making them look like they were a part of his face.

And there it was.

So, I took it.

I took the opportunity.

Just like the two street urchins told me about stealing fruit from Mr. Luchesi's fruit cart: If you think long, then you think wrong. And this time I did not think long nor wrong. Let's just hope the latter part of that street-smart thinking was also correct. While Mr. Gavazzi's nose had the attention of Nikita the Hun, I bolted from the far side of the couch towards the nearest grimy window that gave me a chance to escape. I tried to fling the window open, but it was painted shut. I yanked on it, but nothing. I pulled up harder and then the dried paint started to crack as it separated from the windowsill. Now real panic started to set in as I looked over my shoulder and saw Nikita coming down from his fighting high and remembering what he wanted to do to me. I swear that monster's shirt was going to rip from his thickness. I put my attention back to the window as I heard his fury building up behind me. Push . . . crack. Heave . . . crrackk. TUG . . . SSNAPP . . . SLAMMMM!! The window flew open with the sound like a high-pitched pterodactyl. I flung myself out the window with haste towards wanted freedom. My whole body was out on the dry rotted window ledge, but my head wouldn't budge. It was like my hair was stuck in something. I started to panic and scream. The murderous right hand of Nikita was tangled in my dark hair, and he was pulling me back into that hell hole that I was trying to get out of.

"Vere do you think tink you are going young one?" grumbled Nikita. "I'm just beginning to have fun vit you."

I looked around for help from any of the gawkers at the door, but they had all scurried off in fear like sewer rats being chased by crazed tom cats. The only one left is Mr. Gavazzi laying on the floor with his face looking like a potato. He was in no condition to do anything.

"Come on, my leetle devushka. Let me see if your matb was good teacher to you in how to treat de boarders." I could see the longing in his face and fire in his eyes. God, his breath smelled.

I started to scream in hopes someone down on the street would notice me precariously hanging off the window ledge. The only stable support I really had was Nikita's grasp on my hair. Why is no one helping me? In a neighborhood of more than 20,000 people and not one would help. Maybe word had spread about what happened to Mr. Gavazzi when he tried to help. My screaming led to more screaming which led to wiggling and straining against his hold of my hair. This would be it. If he got me back in the apartment, then I surely would be treated like my mom and possibly killed. He had gotten a better grip on my hair. I could feel the stretching of my skin to the point that my scalp went numb. I kept waiting to be hoisted straight up through the window or maybe my hair to give in to the weight of my body and fall the three stories to my death on the sidewalk. Just as he was getting more frustrated with me, he gave me a hard tug up. I reached up at him to maul his eyes. But instead, I hit my elbow on the windowsill. A few moments ago, I was cursing the rickety window for not working but now I'm singing its praises. SLAMMMMM!!!

Down.

Down came the window.

Right on Nikita's wrist bone just below his right thumb. "AAAAAAIIIIIIEEEEE!!!" Wailed Nikita. Followed by incomprehensible wordage which I'm sure was all Russian profanity.

Nikita reflexively let go of my hair, at least the bulk of it. A lot of it still stuck to his quivering fingers. I fell as he let go of me. I was so scared that I couldn't breathe but I knew that death would come quickly when I would hit the concrete sidewalk.

SMACK!

SLAM!

CRASH!

I fell from the third story window of a four story building and landed on the bright yellow awning that Mr. Luchesi had just bought to protect his fruit from the sun. The flimsy awning did little to break my fall as I rolled off it and onto some metal trash cans that were in a huge trash heap. I couldn't breathe. The wind was knocked out of me. Surely, I had multiple broken ribs, but I didn't care. I tried to get up and out of some type of slime and grime that was someone's meal a few days ago. I had to move and get away. A few people came running over to help but they didn't understand the situation. I needed to get away and seek a copper. I heard a whistle blowing, but I couldn't tell if it was coming from a train or a policeman. Maybe it was coming from hitting my head on a trash can.

"That Bolshevik threw her out of the window up there," someone said.

"No, no she jumped! I saw her with my own eyes. Tried to jump to her death," another said.

"Yeah, yeah! I saw the Russian try to save her!" Someone else added.

"No! He did not try to save me! He was going to kill me!" I screamed as a wave of nausea started to overcome me.

People were starting to stare at me. I begged and pleaded with anyone. "Please help me! My mother was killed in our apartment. Another man was beaten unconscious and the man they call Nikita is trying to kill me." I explained, full of distraught.

"STOP DAT GIRL!!!" Bellowed Nikita from the window. "I SAW HER KEEL HER MATB!! I beg for some-un to hold her until I geet down there. Hold her! I'm coming down." Nikita disappeared back into the room as he made his way down through the tenement building.

I began to stagger along the sidewalk as a couple of drunks moved my way. They were slurring to each other that they needed to stop me for the Russian. "Maybe he'll pay a reward." One slurred to the other. The thought of finally getting away from him just to be placed back into his possession made me want to faint. Another wave of dizziness washed over me.

Fwheeeet. Fwheeeeeeet. There. There it is again. I started around the far corner of my tenement building. I kept looking for the policeman with the whistle, but I couldn't find him. I needed to find him before Nikita found me. Maybe they had finally gone on strike leaving the streets to be overrun by the gangs and thugs.

Fwheeet. Fwheeet. There it was again. It must've been my imagination. I'm a little more than a half a block farther away but it sounded stronger. Suddenly the two drunks from down the block caught up and started harassing me.

"I want something from you, or I'll tell the Bolshevik where you are," slurred the first drunk.

"Well, then imma takin' her first and then imma gonna turn her over to the man and tell him to gimme a reward for catching his girl," garbled the second.

CRACK!! The first drunk fell to the ground. Standing behind him was the policeman, Conor, waving his nightstick towards the second drunk. "Get outta here, woulda. Or you'll be mending goose eggs on your crown just like your friend will surely be doin' behind bars in the morn'." Exclaimed the red-headed copper. The second drunk scurried off in hopes that his feet wouldn't fail him.

"Let me help you up, Elizabeth. My, oh my! What has happened to you, my lass?" he asked.

"LOOK OUT!" I shouted as I saw a dark shadow cross behind Conor but it's too late! Nikita was behind him holding him in some sort of a chokehold. He reached back and grabbed Nikita's grubby beard and pulled hard. Nikita screamed and loosened his grip on him just enough for Conor to slip momentarily out of the hold. I slid away and scampered across the street and paused behind a wooden utility pole. I was trying to decide what to do next. I needed to help Conor but there is no way I could.

"Get over on dat front stoop and vait for me, my devushka. Veen I'm done with dis copper I show you good time. Better time den ya matb ever give to me," grunted the boar as he easily took control of Conor while the policeman was laying on his back. Conor was able to slide his nightstick from his belt behind his back but struggled to raise it toward Nikita's forehead. Nikita was so much stronger and had the upper hand. He pulled it away from Conor as easy as taking candy from a babe.

"RUN, 'LIZABETH! RUN! RUN! RUN! DO NOT LOOK BA . . ." cried the copper. But his sentence was cut short by his own club coming down across the bridge of his nose from Nikita.

* * *

Elizabeth did.

Elizabeth did run.

Elizabeth did not look back.

Elizabeth did not know exactly what happened to Conor. She was pretty sure that she wouldn't be hearing from him again.

She knew she had to go. Go far. But where could she go? How does she leave? Fwheet. Fwheeet. There's that whistle again. It was a whistle. But it wasn't a policeman nor just a sound in her head. That train had been calling her. Calling her to leave this sordid place. This miserable life with little potential. But can she do it? She hated this place, hated her life here. Her mother is gone. Who knew where her father was at that moment? She must leave. Leave or deal with Nikita. She could control her own destiny or allow him to decide her fate. She must be fast and take advantage of the situation. She moved quickly to the sound of the whistle which led her to the nearby rail yard. It was then easy to find an open box car from the train that was making the sound.

The sound of a new adventure.

The sound of a new promise.

The sound of a new life.

The train went over a bump and woke Elizabeth. She must have dozed off for a while. She wasn't sure of the time, where she was, or even where she was going. All she knew was it had been dark for most of the ride. The train had slowed through a couple small towns but hadn't really stopped. She could make out the light from an occasional campfire from the edge of a small woods every once in a while, as the train "sped" past at a blinding speed of twenty-five miles per hour. At least that's what Elizabeth thought she remembered reading from a newspaper last year. Twenty-five miles an hour didn't seem all that fast. But in the pitch black darkness of night with your legs hanging out the side door of a rusty boxcar, you felt like you were floating.

Floating.

A rackety floating.

A rumbling floating.

A clattery type of floating freedom. She always thought floating would be quite peaceful and serene. Apparently, this iron horse that she had hitched a ride upon begged to differ. Elizabeth had been listening to all the train sounds from this boxcar for a while now. It had become quite relaxing in a peculiar way. The noise was its own type of music. After a while she could transform the barrage of noise into some sort of musical sense. The chugging of the engine provided the beat. The banging and clanging of the train's wheels on the steel rails supplied the melody. The wooden slats of the boxcar creaking and squeaking as it rubbed against the steel frame furnished the harmony. Then let's not forget that dang train whistle. That scared the heck out of her. She could never predict when that piercing sound would come. To her, it was just noise. It wasn't part of the music.

In a sense, the whistle represented Elizabeth and her life at that moment.

Unpredictable.

And that scared her to death.

Elizabeth's arm was hooked for balance through a handrail that was on the boxcar door. The last thing she needed was to fall off the train. She had been laying her head against the side of the opened door for balance and the light swaying back and forth of the car rhythmically had put her to sleep. She tried to remember how long it had been since she last ate. Just the thought of eating woke her stomach up. The grumbling and rumbling from the pit of her stomach reminded her that it had been many hours if not more than a day. She started to drift off to sleep once again when suddenly the train whistle blew two long blasts. The brakes started screeching and the train slowed down. She smacked her right ear on the side of the boxcar opening just hard enough to put her on full alert from a disturbed snooze.

Elizabeth questioned herself aloud as tried to make some sense of what was going on, "What is going on? Where am I at? Why are we stopping? What should I do?" She had gotten accustomed to all the sounds of the train, and it had lulled her into a relaxed security. A slight panic about the unknown had begun to set in. Then she heard a rustling sound coming from the other side of the boxcar.

From somewhere within a bale of hay came, "You might as well just stay in here and keep your place unless you're going to jump out and go look for something to eat. We won't be stopping for long."

Elizabeth nearly jumped out of the boxcar when she heard that voice. "Who's there? Where did you come from? How long have you been there?" Her nervous voice filled the boxcar.

"Relax, relax . . . If I wanted to do you any harm, I would have done it hours ago. Now, answer number one," he began, "my name is Leadfoot Frankie and it is nice to make your acquaintance. Two, I come from this country, actually, all over this country. And three, I have been here all my life," Leadfoot then spread out his arms in an awkward bow and smiled exposing tobacco-stained lips and teeth.

"Don't be such a smart aleck," she said, trying to muster as much courage as she could. "That is not your name, I presumed you're from this country and have been here all your life. You know what my questions mean."

"Take a chill pill, Jane. Geez. All I was . . . "

"I don't need a pill!" She interrupted. "And my name isn't Jane!"

"No, No," he laughed, "'Jane' is just hobo slang for a female, which is you," he said. "We hobos don't like to give much information to strangers. That's why the vagueness of the answers."

Elizabeth took a defensive stance and looked around for escape options all the while trying to act like she had control of the situation. "I've been in here for hours. All by myself. I never saw you come in here. So, what I want to know is, how did you get in this boxcar without me knowing it?"

As he started to talk, the train shuttered to a hard stop and that blasted whistle went off again. "We don't have much time to talk if you're wanting to get off and back on again. So once again, I am called Leadfoot Frankie. I've been back here within the bales of hay before you even jumped in. I was taking a pretty serious nap when you bounced in here. You looked incredibly stressed, so I thought I'd let you calm down a bit and I went back to sleep. I guess I slept a little too long. You didn't make any noise or didn't snoop around so I thought you must be harmless. Oh, you've been here for about four and a half hours."

He seemed somewhat innocent, but she didn't want to let her guard down. "With a name like 'Leadfoot' I would have heard you moving around back there and then moving out into the open where you are now." He smiled and just shrugged. "Anyway, do you have any idea where we are?"

Ole Leadfoot seemed to be getting a bit agitated and sighed. "I-I don't know. Some . . . some small tank town. Not quite New York but . . . passed Hartford, Connecticut." Leadfoot pulled out a nice pocket watch and gave it a quick glance. "Listen, we've got about forty-five minutes until this steam hog moves out. We better hop out now and see about food."

Elizabeth didn't know what to do, but she did know that she was starving. So, she decided to go with him. If anything goes wrong, surely there will be someone around to give her help. She jumped out of the boxcar. It was farther down than she thought. She hit the ground and slid on her butt in the rocks, got up, brushed herself off, and stepped over into the weeds to watch the hefty Leadfoot live up to his name. She expected him to drop to the ground with a great force. But instead, he nimbly landed with but a "poof" into the dirt and weeds. Not a blade of grass was creased. His hat didn't fall from his balding head. Even the golden feather that was stuck on the side of his top hat didn't move.

"Leadfoot, huh?" She teased.

"Hey, I never said I lived up to the moniker," he said in jest.

She thought for a moment before she said anything. "So, it's like one of those things that is said but when you really mean the opposite, like calling a tall man 'shorty.'"

"That 'thing' would be called an antiphrasis." He enlightened her with another awkward bow.

She cocked an eyebrow. He shrugged a shoulder. "Don't underestimate a hobo. Just because we don't look like much doesn't mean we don't know nuthin'," He jokingly taunted. Then Elizabeth followed him into town.

She followed Leadfoot into the "tank town." It was a short walk from the tracks and through a small meadow of tall grass to get there. The grass was dewy. She hated dewy. Leadfoot hastily walked through the grass leaving a wake of downed weeds. It made it easier for her to follow him through the knee-high grass. He took about five steps then looked back over his left shoulder at Elizabeth. After doing this a few times he said, "Why are you following behind me like that?"

"Huh? Like what?" she asked.

"Behind me and off to the left. Get up here so we can talk. You're creeping me out a little bit."

Elizabeth kept her distance from him as she sized him up a bit. "Well, I noticed when we were talking in the boxcar that you pulled out your pocket watch with your right hand to check the time when the train whistle blew. You also jumped out of the boxcar by leading with your right foot. That told me that your right hand dominant. If I stay on your left side, then I should have an extra split second to get away from you if you decided to reach for me because you would have to reach across your body to attack me."

Leadfoot stopped and stared at her for a second. "Pretty smart. Sounds like you have been in a couple scuffles in your short life. And also . . . like I told you earlier in the boxcar, if I wanted to do you any harm, I would have done so hours ago when you were nodding off. Not here out in the open. I could've easily given you a shove right out of that boxcar and you would have never seen it coming. But I didn't. Now c'mon have a little trust in me and let's figure out how we're gonna get something to eat. I've shown a little trust in you, and I don't even know your name."

Elizabeth had to admit that there was something about him that was trustworthy. *And well, I'm hungry,* she thought. So, she cautiously moved up next to him but kept her guard up at the same time. "I fully acknowledge that I haven't told you my name. You can call me Elizabeth. But that doesn't mean that's my given name." Leadfoot rolled his eyes at her response. *She is definitely an amateur at this,* he thought. "Just like your mother saw you for the first time and said, 'Oh, look at this beautiful boy. I'm gonna name him Leadfoot Frankie.'" Leadfoot pulled the collar of his jacket up to help hide the grin that was creeping over his face. He could read right through her. She was trying to be so tough earlier and now she was trying to take control of the situation by belittling him. Elizabeth was a textbook scared young lady. He let her comments slide right off him as they walked closer to town. "So why is this called a 'tank town?'" she asked to change the subject. "I've never heard that before."

"A tank town is just a small town that really has nothing in it but a water tank for the trains to re-supply with. Trains don't stay here too long. There's really nothing else here. Very few houses to pick over. We're gonna have to scavenge quickly and get back to the train if we want to get back on it," he explained as they came up to some sort of a shack. Leadfoot seemed to be searching for something on the dilapidated walls.

"Few houses to pick over?" Elizabeth cautiously asked. "Are we about to break into someone's house? Because I'm all for that. I'm all for taking what I need from anyone any time."

Leadfoot gave her a side-eyed glance then to see if she was serious, "No, no, no. We are not breaking into anywhere . . . this time," he added with a mischievous look. He went back to searching around the shack. "Houses lead to possibility and hope. In my experience, possibility and hope lead to finding friendly people. Finding friendly people then leads to food," he said under his breath. "Ah. Here we go. There's the 'mark,'" he excitedly said as he moved a leaning board from the corner of the shack.

"What are you looking for?"

"That!" He said excitedly. He pointed to what looked like a child's scribble on one of the outside walls. No not a scribble. More like . . . a carving. "That is an important symbol for us."

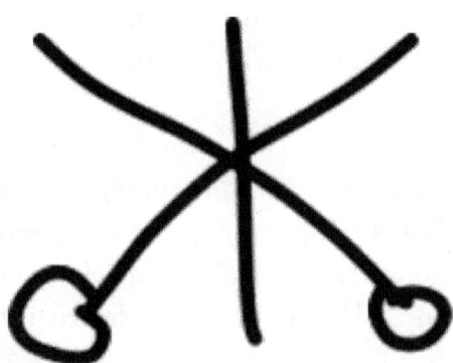

"I am so confused. And hungry. I need food. I don't need to be looking at a child's marking," she said, starting to lose patience as her stomach groaned with hunger.

He chuckled. "This isn't a childish drawing. This is a symbol us hobos use to let other hobos know important information about a certain area. Sort of a code for the road. This symbol, my dear, means that there are fruit trees and/or fruit in a garden nearby."

"Ummmm . . . You're kidding. Right? How? How on God's green earth do those squiggles depict fruit on a tree? Or even remotely a fruit garden?" She was truly bewildered and started to doubt the sanity of her new friend. Her stomach groaned louder this time. Loud enough for Leadfoot to give her a look as if a monster was going to come out of her stomach.

"I'll explain it later. We really need to find these trees, fill our bellies up, and head back to the train. Let's go." Leadfoot grabbed Elizabeth by the hand and hastily led her down a dirt lane that took them behind the only three houses in this community. The houses were widely spread from each other with a small field or maybe more like a huge yard between them. A person would have to shout from one house to the next house to be heard. Each house had a small stable that looked like it would keep a couple of horses or mules with a fenced in area for them to safely graze. She heard dogs playfully barking and birds chirping. Sounds that she didn't hear at all growing up.

Elizabeth had to stop for a moment and stare at these properties. She couldn't imagine living in a place with so much space. This area would be a whole neighborhood from where she was from. "This area could house dozens of families from back home. All this space! I never knew people could have this much space!" She was bewildered.

She suddenly filled up with anxiety. The outer edge of her vision was going fuzzy and unfocused. Thinking about how cramped her living arrangements had been all her life. Dozens and dozens of families jammed and crammed inside a building together for every day and every night. Everyone seemingly on top of one another. Hearing conversations and arguments through all those paper-thin walls. Literally being able to hear the snoring old man from across the hall while she tried to sleep. Her mom allowed her to be in her own room only when there wasn't a boarder renting it. Having to stand in line for the only bathroom at the end of the hall of our floor. Hoping that she could hold it until the other people finish their turn.

"Oh my God!" she said, "I'm lightheaded. I'm having trouble breathing." She started to shake. Her legs got rubbery and then she collapsed to the ground. Leadfoot ran to her, caught her, and guided her to the ground with his thick arms. She looked up at him. He was saying something to her, but she couldn't hear a word. Even her hearing seemed thick and fuzzy.

"Jane! Jane! C'mon Jane! C'mon back, girl," shouted Leadfoot as he lightly shook her. He was trying to decide what to do for help. He was inches from her face. His breath was blowing strands of hair out of her face. He reached in a pocket and took out a handkerchief and fanned her with it. He tried to make her come to her senses as he shook her a little bit more.

"Jane! What's wrong? Answer me!" He shouted as he kept looking over his shoulder towards the woods and then back at the train to see if anyone was around. Finally, Elizabeth started blinking her eyes and catching her breath. The lightheadedness started to fade away.

"I-I don't know," she stammered as she wiped sweat trails from her cheeks and pushed her matted hair away from her forehead.

Leadfoot said, "I think you just had some sort of an anxiety attack."

"Yeah. Yeah, I think you're right. I was having a flashback to back at home." *Is it even my home anymore?* she thought.

"Well, we can talk about it later if we must, but for now . . ." Leadfoot's sentence trailed as he took off down the dirt lane after he made certain that she was okay. Elizabeth picked herself up, fanned her face for a little air, brushed the dirt and grass off the seat of her pants. She looked for Leadfoot and saw him hustling further down the lane. Again, for a nickname of Leadfoot, he moved quite well. She took another glance over her shoulder towards the houses for one more look at the sights and then scurried to catch up to him. Her hearing had completely come back. The birds were still singing and the barking dogs were chasing each other around the nearest barn.

Elizabeth lost track of him for a few seconds as the lane veered off to the left which was not too far behind the nearest house and barn. There was a small grassy field between the barn and the tree line. As she ran around a bunch of bushes, she nearly ran right into the back of Leadfoot. He just stood there quite still and stared at about a half dozen trees. The smell was incredibly sweet. Those trees were exploding with ripe peaches. The bushes that were semi-surrounding them were popping with raspberries and blackberries. What a sensory overload! Elizabeth had never seen fruit "in the wild." The only time she had ever seen fruit was when it was at Mr. Luchesi's fruit stand or when he had them in his cart down at the end of the park where the rich people took their little boat rides in the river. And, of course, she remembered the smell of them rotting in the garbage bags under her bedroom window.

"I have died and gone to heaven," Leadfoot said as his mouth watered. "What a beeeaauutiful site." And with that he got to serious work. He was stuffing all his pockets with the different berries. He was ripping them off their vines not even worrying one bit about the thorns that tugged at his fingerless cotton gloves. In between handfuls that were filling his pockets, he would shove as many berries into his mouth as would fit leaving trails of sweet juice trickling through his stubbled chin. Once he swallowed, he would reach up to the tree and rip off a peach and stuff it into his mouth, not worrying one bit about the fuzzy flesh dripping off his cheeks. Apparently, there were no manners or politeness. Just a sense of urgency.

Elizabeth was still trying to grasp the site of the trees and bushes when Leadfoot urged her to get busy. "C'mon, Jane, quit gawking and get to picking," as he tossed a peach pit to the ground and reached for another. "We don't have much time. We gotta scram real soon."

Suddenly again, she realized how hungry she was. Elizabeth slowly started to pull a couple of berries off a bush trying to be careful of the thorns. "Leadfoot, I'm amazed how you found this. Just from a symbol on an old board. It led us to these perfectly placed trees and bushes. Literally just on the edge of this lane. Why, if I didn't know any better, I'd think that they were put here just for us," she said as bees buzzed around the mature fruit.

"Yes, yes," Leadfoot said impatiently as he took his old felt hat off and started stuffing fruit inside it. "We have to hurry. Are you about ready to leave?"

"Ouch. What? No. I'm not ready. Ouch. I'm not near the expert as you are at gathering these berries," she said as another thorn pricked her hand. I need to get my hands in some gloves. "Besides, won't the train blow its horn when it's about ready? I'd say we have at least fifteen more minutes until the train's horn blows. It'll only take us ten minutes to get back if we walk at a fair pace."

Leadfoot spat a peach pit out of his mouth. He seemed satisfied with the distance that he got from it. "We need to leave now," he said rather suddenly and to the point. "This bounty that has been bestowed upon us didn't just fall into our laps. This garden belongs to one of these houses. I reckon that house right there nearest to us." He pointed at it as he brushed past and reached for her arm to follow him. "There were two black dogs roughhousing in that yard when we got here. I don't see them over there now. I'm willing to bet that they left the yard and are coming right for us!" And then the train whistled.

"I don't understand. Why are they coming for us?" she asked as they started scrambling away from the bushes and peach trees.

"I'm not sure either," said a hustling Leadfoot. His pudgy body swayed left and right while he ran with the extra weight of the fruit. "I would say that we made noise that is somewhat out of character for this area. It's normally quiet around these parts and those dogs probably have radar for ears. Any sound that is abnormal would catch their attention." He looked over his shoulder at the house and pointed. "Look! I see movement in the grass over there. The dogs are coming and they're gaining on us. We gotta hustle for that train!"

Elizabeth was trying to understand how he knew all this. The tall grass in the field between them made it hard to see the dogs. It was especially hard to tell if the breeze was blowing the grass or if the dogs were moving it. They continued running as fast as they could while still holding some fruit. They left the tree line from where the lane was beaten down grass and was now more gravel as they moved closer towards the edge of town. Leadfoot had hoped that the dogs would run towards them through the trees. He hoped that the trees would have slowed the dogs down and would have given them some time, but the dogs took a straighter route towards the edge of the tree line, just missing them by mere seconds as they had just passed through that area. It was as if the dogs knew they would be coming out that way. Elizabeth looked back over her shoulder to get a glance at how close the dogs were. It seemed that the two black dogs had gained a lot of ground on them.

"They're closing in, Leadfoot, I can hear them growling! We're not going to make it to the train! They're gonna be on top of us before we can make it!" She shouted to him.

"Go! Head on down to the train!" Leadfoot yelled back to her. Even though he was much bigger than she was, he was faster. He pointed with his head and said, "I'm getting up on the top of that shack that we were at earlier. I'll try to keep the attention of the dogs while you make your getaway." They got to the shack and skidded to a stop at the back of it. The dogs were about half a football field away and slowing down. They must have thought that Leadfoot and Elizabeth were stuck at the shack and would be easily caught. Their barking and growling were much louder now. You could see their bared canines as they growled. "Here. Take this with you so you have something to eat later." He gave her his hat full of fruit.

Though she had just met him a little while ago, it seemed that she had known him for a lot longer. She couldn't remember the last time anyone had been this nice to her and had helped her like he had done. She needed him. "No, Leadfoot, I don't wanna go without you. I don't wanna leave you here with those dogs! It's not safe for you," she pleaded.

"Life isn't safe. If you always did the safe thing in life then you wouldn't really have a life to live. You would just only exist. And that can't be all that much fun. Now go," he turned her away from him, grasped her shoulders and urged her with a slight push. "Go around the far corner of this shack and run through the meadow towards the train. Keep the shack between you and the dogs so they can't see you as you run. I'll try to keep them busy while you make an escape!" he said. "Count from the caboose forward seventeen cars. That seventeenth one should be a rusty yellow color. Get in that one. That's the one we were in earlier."

"But Leadfoot . . . " she begged as she turned to face him and then slowly walked backwards away from him.

"Go!" He shouted and then added, "Look under the pile of hay bales from where I was when we met. There's a canteen full of fresh water. Take it. I'll be there before the train gains full speed!"

She turned and walked away.

Then the walk turned into a jog.

Then the jog turned into a full-out run.

She made it back to the train with no problems and climbed into the rusty yellow car with little trouble. She then turned back and looked towards the edge of town where she could still see that shack.

Leadfoot had made it to the top of it. The two barking dogs were jumping as they tried to get to him. Finally, one of the dogs found a way to get up on a crate and took a valiant leap and landed on the edge of the shack's roof and was standing just a few feet behind Leadfoot. She screamed for him to look out, but there surely was no way for him to hear her. With luck or skill or both, Leadfoot turned around and with a side-swiped kick to the skull, the mean dog went limp and slid off the roof. It landed with a thud on the ground in an awkward position as dust poofed up around it. The other dog had seen this and stopped barking. It loped over to the dead dog and sniffed at him. He looked back up at Leadfoot and started growling really low and baring its teeth. But instead of charging up to attack him, the dog slowly backed away from the shack.

The train whistled again, and this time the cars clanged and squeaked as it prepared to start the next leg of its journey. The whistle made Leadfoot and the dog impulsively look towards the train. Instead of moving to the noise, the dog just kept slowly backing away. All the way to the edge of the trees. It looked back in the direction of the house and started barking and barking as if something had taken its attention away from Leadfoot. He seized the opportunity and climbed down the back side of the shack keeping it between him and the barking dog. The train hissed from the steam leaving its boiler through the chimney and bolted forward. Man, for a pudgy fellow, that guy sure could move. He was very agile for a big man and proved it as he ran through the meadow. He was close enough now that she could see him look up and count seventeen cars to the yellow one.

"Leadfoot! Hurry Leadfoot!" Elizabeth yelled at him as she waved his hat. The train was moving a little faster now. It was still slow but gaining speed. He made eye contact with her and gave a big toothy smile and started pumping his arms and kicking his legs in an exaggerated form. He must have been confident that he was going to make it because as he ran he put his left hand in his pocket and pulled out a handful of raspberries and smashed them into his mouth.

She started to laugh at him. She hadn't laughed in a long time. She couldn't even remember the last time she laughed. She thought that she may have just made a friend. Come to think of it, she didn't really have many friends. Somehow Leadfoot had created a budding friendship and she was letting him. She had a feeling this journey was going to be quite adventurous with this clown. Maybe, just maybe, luck may be on her side for once. She was concerned that the train was moving faster now. The speed was kicking up a strong breeze. Strong enough to blow her dark hair back off her face. Elizabeth took a look over to this tank town one last time and for the first time in a long time, she said a little prayer of thanks for providing her food and a small adventure with a potential new friend. No. Definitely a new friend.

Elizabeth looked up and saw a tractor coming from way behind the shack and quickly moving their way. Alongside the tractor was that blasted barking dog. There was a man driving the old tractor and he was waving a shotgun. That had to be the man from the house that also owned the fruit trees. Odds were that he owned the dog that Leadfoot killed.

Oh, God, no! "HURRY, Leadfoot, HURRY!!!" Elizabeth screamed as she pointed behind him. He quizzically looked at her then took a peek over his shoulder. Dread fell over his face as he saw the man on the tractor. The man leaned over the tractor's steering wheel and aimed at him with the shotgun. Leadfoot seemed to pick up the pace a little more. She was not sure if it was because the train was moving faster or because the man was pointing a shotgun at him.

"NO!!!! NOOOOOO!!!! HEY SHOOT AT ME!!!" Elizabeth screamed at the tractor. He couldn't hear her over the noise that the train was making plus the noise of the tractor engine. The train whistle screamed even louder than before and longer also. It was loud enough for her not to hear the gunshot that came from the tractor. She could see smoke coming from the end of it. She looked for Leadfoot and feared that he had been shot, but she saw him running back and forth in a zigzag motion as he got closer to the caboose. He was close enough to reach it, but he couldn't. He seemed to be looking for some type of handle to grab.

She looked back at the tractor just in time to see the man aim and pull the trigger again as the tractor bounced through the meadow. Surely, he couldn't have gotten off a good shot. She looked back once again to see if Leadfoot had jumped on the train. He was nowhere in sight. Fear pushed all the joy she was feeling out of her soul as she looked back again and saw the man pump both fists in the air and then pull the tractor to a slow stop. He climbed down off the still chugging and rattling old tractor and picked up the barking dog as it happily licked his face. The man shook a fist and waved the train off in disgust. He then got back on the old tractor still holding the dog and the shotgun and rode towards the houses leaving a trail of exhaust smoke.

The train had now gained full speed.

It was moving fast now. Fast enough that there was no way anyone could jump on it. The summer sun was shining brightly, displaying hay dust floating in the air throughout the railcar. It was starting to heat up inside. As Elizabeth sat on the dusty floor, she remembered that Leadfoot had told her that he had hidden a canteen of water under the hay bales. She went over to the hiding place and easily found it. It was somewhat dented and well used. She twisted off the cap and drank the warm but fresh water. It tasted sweet and refreshing. She took four big gulps, twisted the cap back on, and walked over to a couple of hay bales that were nearest to the open cargo door. She got up on them and laid there propping her head on the canteen as a makeshift pillow. Elizabeth stared out the door towards the sun, breathed a heavy sigh and cried.

4

She didn't fall asleep.

She couldn't fall asleep.

She just wouldn't fall asleep.

A nap wasn't in her. Elizabeth thought about what she could have done to help Leadfoot, but every scenario ended with her also being hurt. She needed a weapon. Something to protect herself. She didn't know where she was going, so she'd have to be smart. Her mom always told her that she had street smarts. Maybe she was right. She had escaped a certain death back home and her street smarts had gotten her to this train. But what then? She was completely vulnerable. If someone who wanted to do her harm was on the train, well, she'd be easy pickings. She had to come up with a backstory. Something that will make people think that she was tougher than she looked.

Elizabeth sat up from laying down on some hay bales and stared out the railcar opening watching the changing scenery. The train started to slow down a bit as the rails seemed to be making a long turn around a bend. The train blew its whistle a couple of times right at the end of the bend and started to pick back up speed.

Just then Elizabeth heard a thump. It came from on top of the railcar. Then another thump and another. She jumped off the bales of hay and hid but kept focused on the sound. Then it seemed like something, or someone was running across the top of the railcar towards the opening. She was certain that someone was going to come through the open door. Ugh. This is why she needed a weapon. All there was in there was hay. Wait! The dented-up metal canteen. The one that Leadfoot had left. That's better than nothing.

Elizabeth quickly scurried across the railcar to its hiding place then remembered that she had put it up on top of a couple of bales of hay. She hurried up there to get it and that's when she saw a shadow. The angle of the sun had elongated the shadow clear through the opening and made it look like some sort of monster was about to jump in. *Oh no! Nikita the Russian. Oh no, no, no! Please God, no,* she thought. *How could he have tracked me here?* She leapt to the top of the bales and found the canteen. It wasn't much of a weapon but it was something.

From where she was sitting, she could see a figure starting down the metal ladder that was connected to the outside of the railcar wall. The figure swung himself through the door like some sort of overweight acrobat that could fly through the air with the greatest of ease. He landed on his two feet with bended knees and with his back towards her. He looked around questioning where he was. Just as she saw his profile, she threw the metal canteen and it hit his left cheekbone and bounced within the bales. Elizabeth had hoped that it had knocked him out but it hadn't. He turned to face her, and she started to scream! "OH MY GOD, LEADFOOT!!!!" She jumped off the bales of hay and landed next to him and gave him the biggest hug she could muster. He returned the hug.

"I thought for sure you were dead," she said in relief. "Whatever happened to you?"

"Well, you see," he began, "I jumped off that shack and took off through the meadow for the train. I have a great fear of dogs and we all know that fear is a great motivator. So, I kicked up my knees so these clodhoppers could get me to my getaway train. I looked up and found you. You were waving at me frantically and I thought that you were afraid that I wasn't going to make the train."

He continued. "That was when I heard a blast from behind me. This wasn't the first time that I've been shot at, so I knew as long as I sped towards the train and outran that rickety tractor I was okay. But that old farmer was a keen shot and I thought something hit my back. But I wasn't sure. Thank goodness for this thick overcoat. I thought it would make more sense to run past and around the caboose and jump onto it from the other side, using the train as a cover. I caught the end railing and foothold at the back of the caboose, swung myself up onto the floor decking, and waved at the old farmer as I ate one of his peaches."

Leadfoot went on, "It took some time getting to you in this railcar. I lost count of the cars. It's easy to do when you're scooting on your rump over the rooftops of a moving train. I would move along the train cars and then take a few minutes to rest. I got a couple of tears in the seat of my pants and in my overcoat from when I'd bang into the side of a car. The material would catch on something. I don't have any physical injuries, per se. Actually, I didn't have a scratch until you threw that canteen at me," he said as he reached up to feel the beginnings of goose egg rising on his cheek.

"Wow, I thought for sure you were a goner, and I would've had to fend for myself without a weapon."

Leadfoot leaned against one of the bales of hay. He looked over and saw his hat that he had given her laying on the floor. It was once full of fruit. He took the hat and pulled out a handkerchief from inside and used it to wipe the sweat off his forehead, then took a full gulp from the canteen. He took a deep breath and sighed then dropped down on the packed hay completely drained. "Man, I'm tired," he said, "I'm not as young as I once was. And yes. You need to get some sort of a weapon."

"Do you have any? I haven't seen you with any."

"Absolutely I do," he said, "this here pocketknife. Oh, and this gut sticker," Leadfoot added as he displayed a nine inch long, thin blade that is slightly tapered to a point. The handle was well worn stained wood. "This gut sticker was granted to me by some bum in Cleveland. It does a mighty fine job in separating meat from the bone."

"You mean as in fileting a fish, right?" she asked.

"Yes, that too," Leadfoot said with a sneer and an arched eyebrow. He took another gulp, drained the canteen and set it beside him. He stared out of the cargo door for a while at the moving scenery. "So, back to a weapon. You're gonna need one. Soon."

A startled Elizabeth answered, "Uh, sure. You're right. But it's not like I can tell the engineer to just stop the train so I can hop off and go buy one. Besides, I have no money. I'm lucky that I was able to run away with shoes on."

"Runaway?" Leadfoot asked.

"No, not 'runaway,' she said. 'Run away.' I'm not ready to talk about that yet."

Leadfoot shrugged, "Ok. Just remember, when you are ready, I'll listen."

After a while of quietly sitting there Elizabeth broke down. It caught Leadfoot by surprise. Of course, he had told her that he'd listen to her, but she gave no inclination that she'd come unwrapped so soon. Burning tears ran down her cheek as she spoke. "I wish all of it didn't happen. I wish I'd killed them all! I wish I could go back and watch them all die!" Leadfoot reached for Elizabeth, but she pulled away from him and went to sit nearer to the door opening. He sat still on the bales of hay and looked at her as she turned her back towards him. Her long dark hair whirling in the breeze.

He gave her a few minutes then spoke, "Learn from it."

"What? What did you say? What do you mean 'learn from it'?"

"I mean learn from whatever you're running from. You just can't forget or even undo what bad things have happened in your life. So just move on and treat it as a lesson learned. Never feel sorry or remorse for your past. Just simply . . . learn. Understand what happened so you won't allow it to ever happen again," Elizabeth turned back towards him and stared over at him, totally bewildered at what he had just said. She wasn't sure she understood. He made it sound feasible. It was like he was talking from experience. "We're all running from something, Elizabeth. Whether it's running into another room in a house or taking a steam train across the country. We're all running."

"Pfft. Running makes you weak."

"Ah, but it doesn't make you weak," he countered.

"Then what does it make you?"

"Strong. And a chance to get stronger. It gives you a chance to catch your breath and to find your strength. Strength for you to help someone else who may have been in the same situation that you've experienced. Strength for you to help give them the choices or encouragements that they may need. And strength for you to go back and face your fears. Strength in finding a way for never allowing the problem to happen again."

She rebutted, "But I think a person needs to confront their problems straight up face to face and be done with it."

"Did you?" He said as she once again turned to face away from him. "I assume not. Why?" She didn't answer immediately.

"Because I didn't have the advantage. Heck, I wasn't on an equal playing field."

"Exactly!" Leadfoot emphasized. "During the Rebellion, the South would lay a surprise attack on the North. Did the North just trudge right through the attack or did they retreat and regroup until they felt that they had the advantage? See what I'm talking about, Elizabeth? Running is not always a bad thing. Just as long as you're looking for the advantage." The more that she thought about it, the more she seemed to accept what he had said, and she seemed to accept that type of thinking.

After a while longer of sitting at the opening, the breeze started to dissipate, and the train seemed to slow down. The train's whistle screamed that something was about to happen.

"What's going on, Leadfoot?"

He was now laying on a bale of hay with his hat resting on his chest. "Sounds like the train is pulling in near the outskirts of a town. They always blare the whistle multiple times when that happens. We'll eventually stop and get on another train if we don't want to stay here. I'd suggest we find an 'accommodation' heading westward."

Elizabeth agreed, "Wow, that whistle sure has caused a commotion. You should see all the people popping up out of the weeds and from behind trees and such. Hey, buddy, stay away from the train. You're gonna get yourself killed," she shouted to someone who thought about reaching for the door frame.

Leadfoot jumped to his feet and quickly moved beside her. He nervously looked at dozens of people looking back at them. The only difference between Leadfoot and Elizabeth and these people was that they were on the train. All the others were trying to figure out how to get on the train. Some of them looked rough. Others looked hungry and dirty.

"I haven't seen this many people at once as long as I've been on the train," said Elizabeth. "Why are they all here and, to be frank, where are we?"

"First of all, you can't be Frank, I am," Leadfoot's attempt at humor fell way short of acknowledgment from Elizabeth. "We must be getting closer to the New York area. I thought it would take a little bit longer for us to get here. It could get a little rough and scary for a while, Elizabeth. This area has a lot of bad people in it. There are a lot of hobos, tramps, and bums floating around here."

"Do you notice any bad people among those that we're passing?"

"I'm sure there are, but I don't recognize anyone down there," he said as he scanned the people. "There's no reason to take any chances. Come here." Then out of nowhere he pulled his gut sticker from its sheath inside his shirt and grabbed Elizabeth.

She was taken aback, "What are you doing, Leadfoot?" She asked in sheer panic. The train started to slow with hesitant jolts. It wouldn't be long until it stopped at its next destination.

"We have to do this quick. You see, you're a girl, a Jane, a bo-ette. Most of the time Jane's are treated awfully good. But sometimes they are handled quite badly," he explained as he took a handful of her long brown hair. "The last few times that I've been in the New York area there was a band of very mean guys causing all sorts of havoc by mostly taking advantage of the weaker men, but especially the Janes." Elizabeth stared at his face as he explained. "I'm sorry, young lady, but this is for your protection." He twirled his gut sticker through his fingers like a majorette twirls her baton and started to hack and chop at her long hair. She was so stunned that she just let him. Let him cut up and cut off most of the long dark hair until it was well above her shoulders but adequately below her ear lobes. As he finished, the train came to a shuddering stop.

Leadfoot let go of Elizabeth as she wildly groped for her hair. "What did you do?" She shouted. "How does chopping my hair protect me from anything?" Her eyes welled up with tears. She wasn't sure if it was from fear or anger.

"Because now you don't look like a girl, a Jane. At least the short hair won't give the impression of you being a female. Listen, if some of these guys know you are not like them then they'll use that to their advantage. You are not safe now . . . but you are safer. We need to hop off this steam hog before we get noticed."

Elizabeth peered out of the railcar door and noticed that no one was trying to get on the train. They mostly just hung out in groups of two or three. A few of them were having animated conversations amongst themselves. Some were just lying in the grass taking a nap. They were easy to see from up in the railcar. She doubted anyone could see them while they were napping in the tall grass. But as she looked out towards the front of the train, she noticed that some of the people were no longer congregating and were moving away from the train.

"Come and take a look-see at this. These people that were congregating at the edge of the train are moving away quite fast." She moved through the railcar to the other side. "They are doing the same thing over here."

Leadfoot had been gathering his few possessions and was putting them in the proper pockets and hiding places when Elizabeth made these comments. He jumped up and grabbed his hat and peered outside of the railcar opening that Elizabeth had just left. "From my experience, the only reason people want to be on the train, then decide not to get on is because of an obvious threat. Looks like we may have a bull or a bo-chaser on our hands."

"Wait," Elizabeth questioned, "a bull or a bo-chaser? What are they? Are they good or bad for people?"

Leadfoot chuckled as he tightened his shoelaces. "Well, it all depends on which side of the problem you are on. The train owners don't want us on the trains illegally for many reasons. So, if you are on that side then they are good. However, if you want to ride the rails, which is illegal by the way, then they can be a force to be reckoned with."

"So, they will come and ask us to get off and give us the third degree. Big deal."

"Ha, ha, ha. Yes, they will ask us to get off and stay off by hopefully using just a club and not a gun. I've seen many guys beaten and some even shot to death. If you don't want to find the wrong end of one of those weapons, I suggest that we go now! Follow me and do exactly what I do. Don't hesitate!"

Leadfoot looked out once again from the one railcar opening then to the other opening where Elizabeth still was. He decided it will be a better, softer landing out that door. He jumped out of the railcar. More like jumped down and out. He extended his legs outward and slid down the embankment. Then he hopped up and brushed the dust and dirt off him. "Easy," he said, "I do believe I looked like Candy Nelson of the New York Metropolitans sliding into second base. Come on now, just like I showed you!"

Elizabeth wasn't as graceful. She jumped up and out instead of down and out which caused her to gain height and came straight down, landing hard in the rocks and rolling sideways to the lower edge of the embankment. She stopped rolling at Leadfoot's feet and looked up at him all dusty and with a couple of cuts to her arms and face. He was trying not to laugh. There really wasn't enough time to do so. He could see someone at a distance coming along the train in a hurry. It very well could be a bo-chaser.

Leadfoot helped her up as she brushed herself off. He looked around and saw that there was a fence that extended as far as you could see under a long row of trees and brush. You could see the small town a few blocks on the other side of that fence peeking out from behind those trees.

"Are you alright, Tumbleweed?" He asked her with a laugh. She picked up a dirt clod, tossed it at him, and nodded. Though she wanted to cry because of embarrassment, she didn't want him to see her cry anymore. "Let's go. I see a part of the fence bent down. We'll crawl over it and head into town."

"Why are we going there? I'm all tattered and dirty," she said.

"That's one of the reasons that we're going. Hopefully, we can find some quick work so we can clean up and maybe get a bite to eat."

"Work?"

"Of course. A hobo earns his daily bread . . . mostly. There are some friendly people here. I know this place well. There's a guy up ahead who owns a small place that has some sleeping quarters out back. He'll feed us for free if we do some small jobs for him. That is if he has any. He's becoming quite popular in helping with our kind."

"Our kind. What is 'our' kind?" She asked.

Leadfoot started to explain as they crossed over the fence. They stopped for a moment so she could pick some dirt out of her chopped hair. "You see, Tumbleweed, you have your hobos, tramps, and bums. Hobos migrate from town to town and pick up work whenever we can. Hobos don't need much. We usually carry a bindle stick that has all our belongings. The tramps are lazy and only want handouts. They don't want to work at all. They will when they are forced to, but they will also high tail it out of town at the first chance. They walk everywhere. They rarely use any transportation besides their feet. Now the bums. They are a whole different breed. Bums do nothing. They don't work. They don't travel. They don't have a home. Bums make us all look bad."

Just as he finished explaining the differences to her, there was a commotion back at the train. They turn around just in time to see a bo-chaser pull a man away from jumping into the exact railcar that they had been in during their journey. That railcar had been her home ever since she left Boston. It seemed to her like a peaceful place. But now the bo-chaser was having his way with that guy. The bo-chaser pulled out a club and beat the man senseless. He picked the man up and stood him against the railcar and proceeded to pummel him some more. Finally, the bo-chaser was breathing hard and was tired from beating the man and walked along the train to find another victim.

They watched the beaten man fall unconsciously to the ground leaving a lot of his blood on the side of the railcar. They looked at each other for a moment, "And that, my dear Tumbleweed, would be what we call 'being on the wrong end of the club.' That . . . is where he lay."

They followed the only road that went into town. These roads were in the early stages of existence. Most towns in this era had roads that were beaten down dirt. Weather was hard on these highly trafficked town roads. Wet weather would make them muddy and hard to travel. Then when a dry period came, the roads would become heavily rutted and left to be beaten down by the shoes of the horses that brought people through the town. Leadfoot and Elizabeth reached this town just after a day's rain left mud puddles in the low areas of the streets. This town was larger than the tank town that they just left. It was also very small compared to living in the crowded, mean streets of Boston.

"So earlier you said that you know where we are," Elizabeth said.

"Yes, we're in a little place called Port Chester, New York," answered Leadfoot. "We're closing in on downtown New York City. But before we go there, we need to get some things worked out."

"Such as?"

"Well for starters we need clothes and when I say 'we' I mean you."

"What's wrong with my clothes?"

"Your clothes are fine, if you're a girl. But I told you, you're gonna be safer if you look like a boy. So, we're gonna get you some clothes. But for now, the first priority is to get some food. Some real food. Meat and potatoes. Maybe even some cabbage." Leadfoot stared out into space just thinking about a possible hot meal. "And I know an establishment where we should be able to get some food. But we're going to work for it this time."

"Well, there is less danger in working for the food. Odds are good you won't get shot," Elizabeth said.

"You're telling me," Leadfoot said as he thought about the trouble earlier that day. "There's a guy that I know that's real friendly to hobos. Like I said earlier he owns a place, a café to be exact. It's just off the main stem of town. We can go there and see what's cooking. Literally and figuratively."

"Main stem?" She asked.

"Yeah, hobo word for Main Street." They reached the downtown area as they passed a livery stable on the east side of the road. Across the street from the livery, they saw four buildings with matching red and green awnings. Three of the four buildings were one story. The one at the corner was a clothing store.

"Is that clothing store the place where we're going to find me some new clothes?" asked Elizabeth.

"Oh no, no, no. You will almost never see a hobo with new clothes. They may be new to him but they're not off the hook. There may be some clothes back in the alley that were discarded. That's where we'll look. I found an awesome hat behind the milliner's store over there a few years ago. But first things first. Food!" They walked past the two-story building and turned the corner as they dodged a couple of more small puddles.

The smell hit them first. The smell of bacon was heavy in the air and was absolutely intoxicating. "I swear I can taste the aroma hitting the back of my throat."

Off the road and boardwalk was a rather large make-shift shanty with lean-tos around the back and far side. You couldn't see inside the lean-tos. They were protected from the weather by old throw rugs and sheets. "I do believe we've found what we were looking for," Leadfoot said with a goofy grin. Elizabeth couldn't understand why they were just standing there.

"What's the deal? Let's go on in. Why are we waiting?"

"Because I don't see a mark. There's no mark anywhere," Leadfoot said as he was scanning the fence posts and a nearby pole. Elizabeth remembered from earlier the mark on the shack that told them that there was food nearby.

Just then an elderly man with a whitish butcher's apron walked out from around the corner of the shanty. He was a wiry-looking man and had probably been pretty agile in his younger years, but now he walked with a slight limp. As he came toward the two, he was wiping blood off his hands with a rusty looking towel. He looked at them over his bent wire rimmed glasses. They, like him, had seen better days.

"It's been a while, Frankie, since I've seen you here," the old man said as a thin smile creased his face. He reached over and patted Leadfoot on the shoulder. "Looks like you brought company this time. What's your name, young lady?" Elizabeth looked up at Leadfoot for affirmation. She thought that she could take down the old man if he hadn't had a butcher's knife dangling out from his side pocket. She wondered how fast he could make a move towards it. He caught her staring at his knife and gave her an open grin and slightly stuck his tongue out through gaps where there should have been teeth. "Come and get it if you want it, missy," the old man said, and then in a flash he had his butcher's knife raised up from his side to shoulder height. Leadfoot jumped in front of Elizabeth.

"Whoa, whoa, now, Gio, there's no harm that needs to be done," Leadfoot emphasized. "I also saw her stare at your blade. I'm sure she wasn't thinking about trying to take it." Even though he was sure that she was measuring him up and trying to decide whether she could take it from him or not. "She's not a threat."

Elizabeth was offended. "Hell, yeah, I'm a threat! Hell, yeah, I was thinking about taking that knife off of him! It would be easy to do! I'm not worried about his quick draw with that knife. I'm not scared of anyone let alone some feeble old man who thinks he's Wild Bill Hickok!"

Leadfoot actually pushed Elizabeth back away from the potential physical confrontation as the old man intently watched what was happening. "Stop! Just stop!" he said to her. "He's a friend who can greatly help us. You are not gonna mess this up for us. You're not as tough as you think you are. We need him! I need him!"

The old man took a few steps back from them and lowered his blade, but he wouldn't put it away. He knew there was no particular threat from this girl, but he had to show some assertiveness towards her just in case. This old timer knew that if you were passive then others would decide your fate for you.

"Gio, you know how it is," Leadfoot stammered. "It's been a long ride on the steam hog . . . "

"I don't care!" the old man interrupted. "Her bazoo is working overtime. I'm not gonna take any guff from a road sister!"

"She's not a road sister. She's more like a tenderfoot. A hungry tenderfoot who thinks that she is Saginaw Joe's sister," Leadfoot explained as he eyed Elizabeth. She started giggling when she heard that comparison. Saginaw Joe was an actual lumberjack that was rumored to be over six feet tall. Now that was huge compared to men at that time who barely stood five foot five inches tall. The legend said that he had huge hands that he brawled with to victory on all occasions. It was said that he also had two sets of teeth that he used to chew off hunks of wooden rails. Folklore of Saginaw Joe would later become the stories and folklore of the original Paul Bunyan.

The old man stared at Elizabeth. "So, you think that you're some kind of lumberjill, eh?"

She wasn't sure how to respond to that, so she just said, "I don't think so. All I know is that they call me 'Tumbleweed.'"

And just like that the old man started laughing. His high-pitched cackle seemed to ease the tension that had risen between them. He cackled and laughed uproariously so much that Leadfoot and Elizabeth began laughing, too. He sheathed his butcher's knife and walked over to the two of them. He wrapped an arm around Elizabeth and said, "Hello. Nice to know your acquaintance,

Tumbleweed. I am Gio Vicci and welcome to my home and labor. Welcome to Papa Gio's Café."

Papa Gio's Café was not what you'd expect it to be. The café/shanty didn't hold many tables. Wooden crates were flipped upside down and used for tables. They were pushed against each other to make the "tables" longer under the makeshift roof. Small rickety benches made out of mismatched two by fours provided a place to sit while you ate. There were six other hobos sitting at the tables minding their business when Gio pulled open the corner flap to show the two inside.

"You never know what there is to eat when you come here," said Gio. "One day it could be soup and then the next day, maybe biscuits and gravy. Every once in a while, a farmer will bring me a goat or a hog to roast over an open fire. Then we would eat on that for days. One time I had a lady bring me five dozen pheasants. Her husband had been out with his friends hunting. They came back home and wanted her to prepare a meal from the birds. They dropped them off and went back into town to finish their three day drunkfest. The wife was so mad that she decided to donate the pheasants to me to feed these men rather than slave over a hot fire for them," he laughed his cackling laugh while he told the story.

He scanned the room of hobos for any potential trouble. Being satisfied that there shouldn't be any, he led them back outside and around the corner of the shanty. "I call this my courtyard kitchen. Outdoor cooking is the best! Today you are in luck. I'm serving bacon, lettuce, and tomato sandwiches with a side of bacon and onion. Gravy is offered if you want it, which I suggest you take. It sticks to your bones."

He handed them each a tin plate and crooked forks. He then led them to a large pan which was setting over smoldering wood chunks with bacon laying there waiting to be taken. The bread looked awfully stale but was not discolored in the slightest. The vegetables didn't look like they would make it to tomorrow, but today was today. Leadfoot slathered gravy over all of it. Elizabeth didn't touch it. This made Gio cackle quietly to himself.

"Haven't been on the road all that long have you, Tenderfoot?" Gio asked.

Elizabeth cocked her head to the question, "What makes you say that?"

"First off, you don't have that road face. Most people that come here has seen stuff . . . "

"I've seen stuff," she interrupted, "I've seen a hobo get beaten up, I've seen a farmer shoot at Leadfoot, I've jumped a train before it took off, and I even had a man attempt to have his way with me after he killed my mom. Do not doubt that I have experiences."

Gio leaned his head way back and loudly cackled. So loud that a couple of guys looked over to see what was so funny. "'A' beaten hobo, 'A' farmer shooting, 'A' train jump, 'A' possible assault. Tenderfoot, let me give you some free advice. Experience is a tough teacher. She gives the tests first then she gives you the lessons afterwards. Just because you got a bunch of 'A's' doesn't mean you learned your lesson." Elizabeth looked at Leadfoot for a clue on how to react to the old man but didn't get any. "How did you get that moniker, 'Tumbleweed?' Is it because the wind blew you into town recently?"

Elizabeth hesitated before she answered. Then she resigned and said, "No, it's because when I jumped out of the railcar I slipped and rolled down the embankment."

Gio slapped his hands down on his knees, leaned up against the barrel full of drinking water and cackled and howled like a crazed wolf. He kept bumping up against the barrel of water as he laughed until it got knocked off its stand. It rolled over on its side on the ground and the water spilled all over. "Don't worry about all that," he said once he got his composure. "There's a flowing creek full of cold water over behind those trees. That's where we get the water."

Leadfoot butted in, "When we are done eating, Tumbleweed and I would like to go fill up the barrel with water. Just tell us where the buckets are, and we will do that."

Papa Gio said, "Ah . . . you remember how this works, Frankie," Gio looked over to Elizabeth. "You see, this place isn't for freeloaders. If you don't have any money to pay for your meals, then you have to work for them. A couple of simple chores gets you a meal. Another couple chores gets you a comfortable place to lay your head. But no more than two nights. I ain't the Astor House and it also ain't no barrel house. Well, not quite as bad as a barrel house but better than a hobo jungle."

Leadfoot and Elizabeth took their plates and went to sit inside the 'café.' "And you wanna know another reason how I know you haven't been around too long, Tumbleweed? Because you didn't take the dern gravy. If you're really hungry, you'll eat anything. Especially if it's free! You'll learn!" chuckled Papa Gio as he went back to finish slicing the rest of the bacon.

"Man, that guy is a piece of work," Elizabeth said to Leadfoot. "He went from wanting to cut my throat to giving me words of advice."

"Papa Gio is rather unique," Leadfoot said between bites of his BLT. "He opened this place up years ago and it's strictly for hobos. He knew there would be times when they needed a place to stay, a place to eat, and really just a place for them to get away from the stresses of the road and rail life. He knows hundreds of hobos that come through here. He helped pass messages from one hobo to another a lot of times. That's how I got to know him personally. Whenever I was down south, I would get word to his family that he was okay. That was until the War Between the States started. It was too dangerous for me to get down there. The train system was not very good there. It was in its infancy. So, I had to pad the hoof. That's hobo talk that means walk."

"Wait, are you telling me Papa Gio isn't from here? I thought I heard a little bit of a southern twang come out, especially when he was getting excited."

"Papa Gio isn't from here. He's from Georgia," Leadfoot added after another bite. "He came up here to work at that clothing store we passed earlier," he pointed at the store while he was chewing. "All the clothes they sold were made downstairs in the basement. He and a couple other people were the only ones that worked down there. How he ended up back here helping out hobos is beyond me. I'm glad he did it though. When the cold winter months come, he will pack up all this stuff and leave it here in a farmer's barn and then he'll hop on a train that travels the High Yaller Line and goes with the birds."

"High Yaller Line?" Asked Elizabeth. "Do you mean like the color yellow?"

"Nope. It's hobo talk for taking a southbound train. You know, as in 'Hi, Y'all,'" Leadfoot said with his gaping tooth smile and then exaggerated a big wave from one shoulder to the other. Elizabeth just stared at him and shook her head in amazement. "What? It's a real thing. Ask any hobo," he said.

"I wonder why he doesn't stay up here all the time. People get hungry in the winter also."

He shrugged his shoulders and finished his sandwich. "I don't know. I guess that's just his thing. Here he comes now. Ask him yourself."

Papa Gio walked by with a couple of heads of lettuce in his hands. "Hey, Gio!" Elizabeth yelled towards him after she swallowed a big bite. "Why do you go south for the winter? I would think you would be here all year providing food and shelter for people."

He stopped and responded, "You ever spend most of the day freezing your toes off for the sole reason of having to keep stirring the soup so it will stay warm and not freeze? Have you ever been so cold that no amount of blankets and quilts could keep you warm? I bet not. I bet you always have had a roof over your head, eh Tumbleweed? I'd risk to say that you always had food too, though, it may never have been enough. Well, let me tell you something. I guess it's my calling to be here and help those who need help when I can. I feel like people helped me when I was traveling all over this country looking for work. I was lucky to find it."

Gio leaned in towards Elizabeth and lowered his voice, "The family I had left I loved, and I was running from something that led me here. I praise the good Lord Almighty from up above that He provided me with this opportunity of helping people. It just happened to be here, not back at home. When this parcel of land opened up and the farmer down the road let me borrow it, well, it was a blessing in disguise to help these people. That blessing provided me this place to do so. So here I am. And when the wind blows from the north, then south is where I'll be. Because I don't eat snowballs."

After a while, Gio was able to give the two some chores. This provided them an extra meal and a semi-private place to sleep. Elizabeth and Leadfoot both carried buckets of water from the creek back to the water barrel to fill it back up after it had been spilled. Leadfoot carried and stacked a rick of wood that was chopped earlier in the day by another hobo. Elizabeth was tasked with stacking the clean plates and utensils that another hobo had washed and dried. After that she had to fold and stack clothes that had been donated, cleaned, and washed. She thought about taking a shirt and a pair of trousers when no one was looking but thought better of it. She didn't know who she could really trust while she was here. So, she decided not to trust anyone and left the clothes. The evening meal was soup, beans, and more bacon. Chunks of torn up bread were offered as well and, of course, gravy. And, yes, Elizabeth poured on a lot of gravy this time.

The bunks were semi-private. Gio said that it was for each individual's protection to have a bunkmate. He believed that it would be harder to rob someone if there was another set of eyes nearby. "No one should be by themself. They should always have someone around," he said. Papa Gio took them to their spot for the night. It was separated from the others by hanging sheets used as partitioned walls. There was a cot on each side of the room. Each cot had a blanket but no pillow. The ground was covered with hay so they wouldn't be standing in mud or on dirt.

There was even a dilapidated nightstand with two drawers in between the cots so each person could put their belongings in there if they wanted to. Most people just kept their things in bed with them so they would not get stolen. Elizabeth didn't have anything but the clothes on her back. She was surprised to see that there was a very worn bible with a bunch of pages torn out in the top drawer.

Gio stopped by to make sure everything was sufficient and also had a list of chores that would need to be done in the morning. He let them look over the list and had each pick two chores. "There may be other chores that need to be done. I have fewer people staying tonight than usual. I suspect that a couple will skip out at first light tomorrow to catch a ride to the Sacred Tract Road."

"Sacred Tract Road, huh?" Leadfoot asked Gio as he watched for any expression from Elizabeth. "That's the steamer to Boston, ain't it, Gio?" Elizabeth looked up at Leadfoot and Papa Gio as they talked. Gio didn't catch on to what Leadfoot was asking, but Elizabeth did.

"Well, duh, Frankie. You should know that. Your brain's turning to mush with that rail bouncing you've been doing," said Gio. "Ah well, the wash tub will be in use tomorrow. Though it will be chilly in the morning, I suggest you get in quick and early before the other six get up. I'd hate to be the one that had to use it after all you jokers. Might just as well take my chances in the creek. That water will sure be cold down there. Frankie, I'll fetch you a blade so you can scrape your mug. Looks like it's been a few days since that face has been bare of bristles."

Leadfoot said, "Gio, I started to ask about the mark earlier when we showed up."

"What mark do you mean? The one on the fence picket?"

"Yes."

"Well, I'm not too sure about that," said Papa Gio. "What I do know is that there is a couple of new cops here in town. That picket had been removed a time or two and I had to replace it. The rumor is that they don't like this establishment because of the tramps and bums coming around. They don't know the difference between them and hobos. When the bums and tramps show up here, I directly send them on their way. I don't know if they caused a scene in front of the cops or what. But I've sat down with a couple other coppers, and they seem to understand that the bums and tramps are not our people. So, who knows? But I do know that y'all are safe here."

Leadfoot and Elizabeth slept as well as expected on the cots. It was still early but you could see dark sky turning gray due to the first light. Leadfoot rolled over on the cot and sat up still wearing his clothes. He looked over at Elizabeth's cot and it looked like she had melted into it. The blankets were rumpled but completely flat on the cot. "Elizabeth?" he whispered. "Tumbleweed?" He got up off the cot and walked barefooted through the thin layer of hay over to her cot. It was empty. He pushed the canvas corner aside as he went out of their room. Just then he heard the whistle. The whistle for the steamer heading on the Sacred Tract Road. A part of him thought that she had snuck out and gone on that train back to Boston. He didn't know the whole story of why she had left in the first place. He could piece it together with what he had picked up so far from her. He couldn't blame her if she went back. It's human nature to seek out revenge during a time of suffering. He just hoped that Elizabeth wasn't thinking illogically and planning to go.

"Better get in that tub," Elizabeth said as she startled him. "I got up early and Gio already had a fire going under it. Does he ever sleep? I was the first to use it. Well, after Gio, of course. He took my clothes and said that they'll be washed and ready for me by the end of the day. Though I have a feeling I'll be washing my own clothes. I think he added that to my chore list. I saw two other guys walk that way and thought that I'd have to wait until they were done using it, but they kept walking. I'm assuming they headed off to try to hitch onto the train."

"And you didn't follow them to the train?" he asked.

"No, of course not," she proudly answered. "I didn't even think about it. I knew you would think I'd go back and seek revenge. But I thought, I've only been on the road for a few days. I understand that there will be dangerous days ahead of me out here. But if I go back, there are going to be even more dangerous days for me. Guaranteed. At least right now I'm nowhere near my problems from my recent past. I'm free. I'm free to go wherever my nose leads me. This is all I got right now. This is all I want right now. This is what I need right now. It may be for a week. Then again it may be for a year. All I know is that right now, at this point in time, I'm having fun."

"How old are you?" Leadfoot asked in amazement. "You have the look of a kid, but you have the thought process of an adult."

"A girl never tells her age. But I am tough. Tougher than I should have to be . . ."

The rest of the day was uneventful. There were only four of them left and four more came straggling in the café. Every one of them seemed to know Papa Gio and all were respectful to him. He seemed to know each one as well.

Papa Gio went up to Elizabeth while she was taking some clothes off the line. "Here. You're going to need these." Elizabeth looked down and looked at the clothes that had been given to her. They were not new, but they were new to her. At least they didn't have holes or rips in them like the ones she had been wearing.

"How am I going to carry these things?" She asked.

"Simple. Here's a large pillowcase. Put your clothes and other belongings in it. Take this stick," he gave her a stick that was hand carved out of a hardwood, "and tie the pillowcase corners to the stick like this. You now have a bindle and a bindle stick. You are now a genuine bindlestiff."

She thanked him with a huge hug and a big smile. "There's a little surprise about that bindle stick of yours. Look at the bottom end of it," he said.

She looked at the bottom end of it. It looked like it could come off. She tugged hard and the end did pop off, exposing a three-inch blade coming out of the end of the stick.

"You need a weapon. A stick is a good weapon but since you're a female you need extra protection. This will keep the four-legged wolves and also the two-legged wolves at least five feet from your person."

"I-I don't know what to say, Papa Gio," she stammered. "You have provided me a lot with these small gifts."

"Yes, I guess they are small gifts, if you don't think having clothes and protection are all that important. You need to be careful."

A cleaned shaven Leadfoot walked up to them as they were speaking. "I hope I'm not interrupting anything," he said.

"No, nothing personal. I was just giving Tumbleweed her bindle stick and some personal items she'll need," as he gave her a slight wink. "There is another thing I need to give you and that's a better haircut than the chop job you have now."

Leadfoot started laughing as Gio came up with a pair of scissors. After about a half hour he gave Elizabeth a cracked mirror to look through. She was sad but understood that this was needed. It actually didn't look that bad. Papa Gio had cut it even higher off her shoulders than Leadfoot had done in the railcar. He smoothed up all the choppy stuff from where Leadfoot got ahold of it.

Later on in the late afternoon they had supper. Leadfoot and Elizabeth had spent the entire day doing odd jobs for Papa Gio. They both felt that it was the least they could do for all that he had done for them in the last two days. "So, what's the plan for you guys?" Gio asked.

They both stared at each other for a moment then Leadfoot said, "Well, you know how it is on the road, Gio, you always have time to have somewhere to be. I think I'm gonna let Tumbleweed here make that decision." Both men turned to her and waited on a response.

"Keep going the direction that is as far away from Boston as I can get. That's simple enough. When does the next train leave?"

"There's an accommodation heading west at daybreak tomorrow. I know it goes through the Big City down the line. I'm not sure after that," Gio said.

"There we go," she said, "we'll be ready for it. Where's the best place to wait?"

Leadfoot spoke up, "Hold on just a minute there, Tumbleweed. There are some things you don't understand. You don't just 'wait' for the train and 'jump on' when the timing's right."

"Yeah, it may end up being on a bad road and you'll have to take to padding the hoof," added Gio.

"Ha, ha. I know what padding the hoof means. Leadfoot told me that yesterday. I'm getting to know the lingo. I bet a bad road means that the road has a bumpy track or has many delays," she said.

Both men looked at each other for a second then Leadfoot spoke up again. He had taken on an even more serious tone. "No, Tumbleweed. A bad road is when there are trainmen that could be exceptionally hard on us if they found us. To the point where they may kill us or, even worse . . . they don't." Silence filled the shanty. These men had seen stuff. "This life is seriously dangerous, Elizabeth." She noticed that Leadfoot called her by her name and not her moniker. He must be serious.

Gio said, "We're gonna have a full night here tonight. I suggest you two get back to your spaces before trouble arises. I've had too many quiet nights in a row. I'm due to have to break up a skirmish or two. You good people need to go. I'll try to see y'all off tomorrow. But no guarantees."

And just like that they were back on their cots. There was no breeze that night. Elizabeth wanted to pull the canvas back so they could get some air, but Leadfoot wouldn't allow it. There was too much movement around the lean-to that night. Opening up the canvas would invite someone in. Soon after the stars popped out and the cicada's sang 'reee-uhhh, reee-uhhh, reee-uhhh,' Leadfoot was sacked out. Elizabeth laid on her cot with a light sheet over her to keep any bugs off. She held her bindle stick by her side with the pointy end facing the canvas waiting for someone to peer in.

Gio had been right with his feeling that he was gonna have to knock some heads during the night. He rarely wanted any police involvement. So, he would take care of all the troubles. He broke up two fights. Banishing all four guys away from his hobo café to fend for themselves out in the woods or having to take their chances in town with the police walking the beat. In the wee hours of the morning, Gio had laid out a couple of nose bags for Leadfoot and Elizabeth just in case he missed them leaving.

Elizabeth laughed when Leadfoot called the sack lunches "nose bags." She certainly understood why they were called that when the first thing she did was to open it up and stick her nose in to smell what was in there.

The sun was rising in the east and Leadfoot and Elizabeth started their walk south towards the track. They decided against walking through town this time. They didn't want any hassle with the police, so they walked the outskirts of the small town. As soon as they left the café property, they heard someone yelling at them. It was Papa Gio. He was yelling for them to stop. So, they did and waited for him.

"I was doing some thinking last night after I busted up the last fight," Gio said. He looked like he may have taken the short end of the stick in one of those fights. His left eye was in the process of being closed off rather than being open. He looked at Elizabeth and explained, "Tumbleweed, I want you to come back here the next time you're in the area. And I also want you to have some extra protection. So, I'm gonna let you borrow my meat cleaver that you were eyeing so much when we met. Borrowing it means that you have to bring it back. You got it?" He gave her a snarling look. But it was okay because she knew that look was just as good as a hug and a kiss from this man. She accepted it and tied the sheath around her shoulder and cleanly slid the cleaver in. Then off they went towards the track.

When they got to the track area, she couldn't believe her eyes. There were no other hobos. There was nobody around at all. There was no train. There was nothing at all. "What the heck? Where the hell is the train?" An astonished Elizabeth asked Leadfoot.

"I do not know. Could be a dozen reasons. It could be something big like an accident of some sort, or in all actuality, it could be that we simply just missed it. I guess we need to point our toes west and let us take to padding the hooves. Maybe a steam hog or a battleship will find us."

So off they went with the sun coming up over the horizon at their backs. It was trying to dry the dewy grass as much as it could. Leadfoot and Tumbleweed continued their travels with Tumbleweed's pointy end of her bindle leading the way.

The sun was beating down on Elizabeth and Leadfoot for most of the day. So much so that Leadfoot had taken off his topcoat and put it on his head to keep the sun off his neck. He used his hat as a basket to place the random berries he found growing wild along the railroad track. Elizabeth had planned on braiding her hair and tying up the braids until she remembered that Leadfoot had chopped off most of the length. She gave him a sour look when she had brought up that topic a few hours ago. He just grinned and shrugged.

The sun was pretty relentless on the two souls as it beat down on them in the late afternoon. "Why don't we just walk in the cool of the night instead of this heat?" Elizabeth wondered.

"I don't like to walk in the dark too much," Leadfoot said. "Too many creepy crawly things around. Two legged and four legged. If something bad happens it's usually in the dark. That's one of the reasons why Gio wanted us to stay put when those ruffians came to his place."

"Leadfoot, I feel bad for not helping out Papa Gio in those tussles he got into. He was so good to us. We should've helped," She remembered the bruises on his face.

"If he needed our help, he wouldn't have asked us, he would've told us. Gio's been around. He isn't afraid to jump in a fight or two. He knows his limitations."

"Yeah, but the look of that eye and his staggered gait suggested to me that he had some shortcomings exposed." Leadfoot nodded and chuckled in agreement as he fumbled with something that he took out of one of his inside coat pockets. "What is that?" She asked. Leadfoot pulled out a harmonica.

"It's a harmonica that I found lying around at a hobo jungle a few weeks back," he said. "I got to know this guy. He was some type of musician, at least I thought he was. He was pretty good with a fiddle. The night that I found the harmonica, it was lying next to a log. I presumed that someone had been sitting there and bumped it off the log or someone had just lost it. So, I looked it over. I knew what it was, but I had never played one before. I put it up to my lips and blew. I think all the music had been blown out of it because all that was left in there was some foul notes. Man, that sound was atrocious."

Leadfoot continued, "Then this guy came from out of nowhere and asked me if I knew that I was supposed to play it with my mouth and not my nose. We both laughed and laughed. We hit it off really well. That's when he told me that his name was Joe and he was from Illinois. He was just wandering the countryside and doing odd jobs. Most of the jobs were playing the fiddle in parks and saloons for food or cash. He pulled out a fiddle and played a few tunes for me and some other hobos that had been passing by. It was getting late so he told me that if I didn't mind the company, he'd travel with me in the morning and teach me how to play the harmonica. He said that if he could teach his son how to use it, surely, he could teach me."

"When I woke at dawn, Illinois Joe was gone. I never saw him since. I wondered if the thought of teaching me how to play it reminded him of his young son." Leadfoot never blew in it. He just looked at it and stuck it back in a pocket. "I guess if I'm in need of a quarrel, I could pull the harmonica out and blow into it and make it sound like a duck quack for the afternoon. That would surely get someone roused up to fight."

"You ever been in a bad fight, Leadfoot? I bet you have some awesome stories."

He hesitantly answered, "Yeah. Many. I prefer not to talk about them though, Elizabeth. Like I've said before, you have to understand that this life is dangerous and even more dangerous for a female. There will come a time in this lifestyle that you have to prove the worth of your word. Sometimes it's as easy as being forceful with words, other times it's using force with hands."

"So, you're saying most of the time actions truly speak louder than words," Elizabeth got a few nods from Leadfoot as it seemed his mind had wandered a bit. "Well, I think if some problem comes to me, I'll end it before the talking starts," she added.

"You have to remember that your word is your honor. If you have no honor, you have no help out here. Always start off using nice but forceful words. If that doesn't work, then relent to force. When you do this, they will believe your good intentions with the words. If you start with force, then no one will believe the nice." Leadfoot hoped that Elizabeth understood his quick lesson as he saw her mulling over his words.

Elizabeth started thinking about the situation that she had with Nikita and what possibly would've happened if she tried to talk her way out instead of fleeing. After a few moments she said, "But there is always an exception to every rule." Leadfoot stared out towards the rails as he pondered her comment. He didn't answer her.

The humidity was becoming unbearable. The air was heavy with moisture.

"I will say, Tumbleweed, it's so humid out here that my underclothes are getting up close and personal with me," he declared as he wiped the sweat off his head with a handkerchief.

Elizabeth waved her bindle stick around after she took off the end cap exposing the blade. "If you look real close, Leadfoot, I think you can actually see me cutting the air."

She put the cap back on and sat on the rail for a moment. "I'm hungry. What do you think about opening up these nose bags and resting for a spell? A nap may sound good also. Maybe it'll cool off as it gets later."

"Sounds like a splendid idea. Let's wait until we get to that bunch of pine trees and sit under them. They'll provide a lot more shade," Leadfoot said as he pointed towards the trees. They ambled towards the clump of pines. Luckily, it took them only a few minutes to get there. The air was slightly cooler when they were under trees. They plopped down and opened their nose bags. The smell of salty bacon lazily floated from the bags. Also, inside was some brown sugar, two pieces of beef jerky and a handful of uncooked rice and beans. Leadoff had a few blackberries left over from picking as they walked the rails. "Let's hold off on eating the beans and rice. They'll be better over an open fire."

"Sounds good to me," she said as she gnawed on a piece of jerky. "It's too hot to start a fire anyway. We need rain. It needs to rain right now," she groaned. "I hope that it would get cooler if it rained." Leadfoot just scowled at her. "What? Why are you staring at me like that, Leadfoot?"

He swallowed a piece of bacon then said, "You jinxed us, Tumbleweed. You never beckon the rain gods for them to do their magic when you're a hobo. We might as well just make camp here for the night."

"Wait a minute," she said as she heard a low rumble coming from the direction they just left. "There's no such thing as rain gods! Or is that some hobo code that you're gonna explain to me? Wait! Before you answer, is that a train that I hear coming?"

Leadfoot responded, "Nope, that ain't no train." He took a long swig from his dented canteen. "That's angel's bowling balls crashing into their pins. Unfortunately, it sounds like we're gonna get a gutter ball of weather coming our way." He got up and summoned Elizabeth to get up too. "C'mon, time to turn that sticker into a cutter and put her to good use. You need to cut down some branches from those pine trees on the outer edge and bring them in here so we can lean them against these trees for shelter. I'm gonna go search for dry wood for a fire just in case we have to stay here long."

"Why can't I go search for dry firewood and you cut down some branches?"

"Because you're the one with the cutter, Tumbleweed, no one else should use your weapon but you," sighed Leadfoot and then pointed up to the developing dark clouds. "Besides, you're the one that poked those bowling-angel-rain-god-things up there."

It rained.

It rained long.

It rained a long time.

It rained for the rest of the afternoon and well into the next day. In fact, Leadfoot and Elizabeth didn't even think about venturing out of the makeshift lean-to until late afternoon. The rain had washed away most of the humidity but left a promise of its return a near certainty. Their little lean-to was very adequate. It was small, but it had provided space for each of them to stretch out without bothering the other. Leadfoot showed Elizabeth how she could catch some of the rainwater and then use it to cook some of the beans and rice. To pass their time during the storm they mostly rested with a lot of tale-telling. Leadfoot had many tales to tell. Elizabeth found out that his life as a hobo was actually a quiet one. He mainly stayed away from large towns and remained in the countryside over the years. She didn't ask why. She was learning not to ask too many questions and to just listen to what stories he had to offer. She was able to tell a few stories of her own pertaining to how noisy her life had been in her neighborhood where she was raised. She stayed away from any conversation about her family, though, just like Leadfoot had shied away from some of his personal stories and wild tales. She never realized how noisy her life had been back home until she had experienced some of the quiet and solitude out on the rail.

The rest of the afternoon lingered on into early the evening with not much to do. They washed a few of their clothing in some of the rainwater that they had caught earlier that afternoon. By now, all the clothes were dry and Leadfoot seemed to be getting antsy. "It looks like it's gonna be a peaceful night. So, what do you think about us cleaning up this place and packing up our stuff?" he asked her. "We can sleep under the cover of stars tonight and then get up in the morning for an early start."

"To where?" She got up and started to clean up some of the debris that was left from their lean-to.

"I don't know," he answered. "I guess westward, though, I'd rather not stay in the Big City." Just as Leadfoot had begun his next sentence he heard a rustle coming through the edge of the trees.

"Well, what do we have going on here?" A slender man said as he stepped out of the tree line. The slender guy looked like he had missed quite a few meals. His face was gaunt, but his clothes didn't really hang off him. They clung to him exposing a lean wiry physique. One other guy followed behind him. He was shorter than the slender guy and had a squat and thickset frame. His threadbare clothes threatened to fall apart at the seams at any moment. The shorter one was trying to get a look over the slender guy's shoulder to see what he was looking at. When neither Leadfoot nor Elizabeth answered the slender man's question he asked it again, but with more intent.

Leadfoot replied, "We don't want any trouble. There's nothing going on here, and we don't have anything of value. You just need to move along."

"Move along?" The slender man soberly said. "Or what?" Elizabeth and Leadfoot lost sight of the shorter thickset man as he walked back into the trees and seemed to be moving around behind them. "OR WHAT?!" The slender man yelled. You could hear his shout echo through the trees.

"Or you'll die right there where you're standing." The slender guy and Leadfoot both turned their heads toward Elizabeth as she took a defensive stance and pulled out the cleaver that Gio had given to her. A long greasy smile slowly formed under the slender guys pointed cheekbones as he turned his attention to Elizabeth.

"Tumbleweed . . . " warned Leadfoot as he cautiously looked for the shorter man, trying to anticipate where he may pop out. Years ago, he had come up with a weapon system. He had knotted small dagger blades to a rope and then looped the rope from one forearm, around his shoulder blades to the other forearm. He was able to keep them hidden under his shirt. He could then slowly roll his shoulders forward so the two blades from his long shirt sleeves could fall to where the handles were just under his thumbs. He sensed that this was a good time to use them. Nothing good was about to happen now.

"A bo-ette…Interesting," he mumbled almost to himself. "I did not see that coming. Tumbleweed, eh?" The slender man quietly taunted as he gazed at Elizabeth. He was sizing her up. He slowly lifted up his left arm and pointed a long index finger at the cleaver that Elizabeth was holding in front of her. "That's a rather daunting specimen for a bo-ette to be flinging around." He slowly raised his right hand and pointed his index finger at Leadfoot. "You, my good man, need to take a seat on your filthy trousers and keep those thumbs pointed up to the heavens." And with that comment he flipped a switchblade from out of thin air and threateningly pointed it at Leadfoot. It looked rather new. Maybe recently stolen from a store or from another person. The blade picked up the reflection from the dying campfire. Leadfoot hesitated but slowly sat down like he was instructed to do. The slender man turned his dark face back to Elizabeth. "Gimme that cleaver," he directed. "GIMME THAT CLEAVER RIGHT NOW!!!" He yelled.

"You need to step back and leave us alone," she demanded. "We've come from back East and are heading out West. We don't mean any harm to anyone. But if you don't leave us be, I won't hesitate to kill again."

The slender man stared at Elizabeth a little longer and didn't say anything. He was not too concerned with Leadfoot at the moment because he knew his shorter thickset buddy was just a few feet behind Leadfoot and if he as much as flinched, the slender man knew his buddy would drive a knife through the back of his neck. Leadfoot seemed to sense the same thing as he heard a twig snap a moment ago from behind.

"You are an intriguing one aren't you…Tumbleweed?" The slender man said as he held his gaze on her and kept his fingers pointing at the two of them. "I want that cleaver. And everything else you have."

"Go ahead and look at what all they have," said a voice just behind Leadfoot. "This ole guy ain't goin' nowheres." The shorter man poked the point of a thick blade just under the base of Leadfoot's skull. He knew one quick move and he'd be a goner. The slender man slowly took a couple of steps over to their makeshift lean-to and started rummaging through their stuff.

"Trash. Nothing but trash here," he said with disappointment in his voice, "and all that they have is just useless junk. How in the world do you live and survive with this junky garbage?" he asked himself quietly. He then looked back to Elizabeth and the cleaver. The slender man took a couple of slow steps towards Elizabeth. Leadfoot leaned slightly as if he was thinking about making a move. The smaller man had anticipated that and pushed the blade slightly deeper into his scalp.

"Easy there, big guy. You's start leaning like that again and we'll see how much deeper this blade will go into the back of your skull."

"I think it's time for me to take that cleaver," the slender man said to Elizabeth. She gripped the handle of it a little tighter and wondered if Papa Geo would be ashamed of her if he found out that she lost it. Lost it in less than a couple of days. She looked over at Leadfoot as he was down on his knees. She felt that she had to do something quickly.

"You might as well take the cleaver. It's a murder weapon. I'd hate to get caught with it anyway," she said as nonchalantly as she could. She tossed it to the ground by the slender man's feet.

The slender man watched the blade slide to a stop near his boots. He looked back up at her slowly and asked, "Murder weapon, you say?" as he gazed into her eyes. "Do explain."

"Yeah, murder weapon. That's what I said. Go ahead and take it, sucker," she began. She remembered reading in the newspaper the morning before she left Boston of a murder of a woman in Rahway, New Jersey. A woman was found under a bridge near a river. Police thought that she may have been a prostitute. "I met this woman in

Rahway, New Jersey, that's where I'm from," Elizabeth lied, "and I passed by her on the bridge. She was carrying a basket full of eggs, and I was hungry and wanted them. She wouldn't give 'em to me so I punched her in the face and then took that cleaver that's at your feet and sliced her face not once, but twice. She dropped the basket, and I pushed her off the bridge to her death." Elizabeth was rather proud of her storytelling. The slender man stared at her during her story as he folded his arms in front of himself.

"Tell me," he said, "what color of a dress did she have on?"

"Green. Dark green," she answered.

"Did she wear gloves?"

"Yes, as a matter of fact, she did. Yellow ones," she was curious where these pointed questions were going.

"I believe you. I believe you came from out East," he said. "We've been watching for a train to come out of the East and to take us on that new rail to California for the last few days now. You see, we're making our getaway. The information you told us is exactly correct. So correct, that it's like . . . you read it in a newspaper. But let me give you some information that wasn't in the papers. The woman's left hand was cut off for no apparent reason. But I know the reason."

Elizabeth's courage was draining out of her. "Why?" She asked.

He began, "Because, she scratched my neck when I grabbed her to throw her off the bridge after I was done using her." He pulled back his shirt collar and jacket to show three long red marks on his neck that were becoming scars. "Then I hurried down to where she laid and cut off her hand for a souvenir." Then he reached inside his jacket pocket and pulled out a rag that was wrapped around a badly decomposed hand and showed it to Elizabeth. "You see, Tumbleweed, I'm one of the best, if not THE best, at what I do. And what I do is not very nice." He picked up the cleaver at his feet and pointed it at Leadfoot. "My good man, I'm going to do you a favor. I am going to take this little bo-ette from your custody being that she's the only thing of worth you seem to have here. But don't worry. First, I'll release you from this life, so you won't have to see the nasty things we'll do to her."

Elizabeth picked up her bindle stick as if she was accepting her fate to go with them after they killed Leadfoot. Then all of a sudden, Leadfoot fell forward. Right on his face. Elizabeth screamed! She knew that he fell forward from being stabbed in the back of the head by the shorter guy.

"Well, what in tarnation," said the shorter man, "I didn't touch him. He must have fainted at the thought of his demise." Leadfoot then quickly flipped over onto his back and with the two blades that he had in his hands he reached up and poked both blades into the eyes of the shorter guy. The shorter guy fell on top of Leadfoot as the life was pulled right from him. The slender man had the cleaver in his hand. He was taken aback at what just had happened. It was not supposed to happen that way. He threw the cleaver at Leadfoot like an Indian throwing a tomahawk. The cleaver completely missed him and stuck into the side of the shorter guy's shoulder.

The slender man pulled out his own blade and looked threateningly at Elizabeth. She already had her stick in her hands ready to use it. The slender man started to laugh, "That stick is all you have to protect you? This is gonna be too easy." As he finished his sentence,

Elizabeth pulled the wooden cap off the end of her stick exposing the blade. She swung it out towards the slender man and caught him on the right ear. He reached up to his damaged ear and she swung the blade to the opposite side of his head and plunged it into his neck right between the scratches from the hand of the Rahway woman. As he fell down to his knees, you could see the surprised look on his face give away to the acceptance of his fate. Never did he think a girl with a hidden blade in a bindle stick would be able to take him out of this world. That was the last thought that went through his mind.

"I almost waited too long, but I did just like I said, Leadfoot. Remember earlier when we talked about your word being your honor?" Elizabeth asked as she was trying to be strong, but she couldn't overcome having a shaky voice. "My word is my honor. I told him I'd kill him, and I did." Then she dropped her bindle stick and watched it fall and land directly between her feet. She slowly sat down and stared at the slender man's dead body.

Death came quickly to those two guys that night. Elizabeth stayed sitting on the ground crossed-legged as Leadfoot moved the bodies to just inside the edge of the trees. He used the dead men's blades to loosen up the dirt to dig shallow makeshift hobo graves. He had asked Elizabeth to fetch as many rocks and gravel as she could to help cover the graves, but she didn't move. He didn't press her on the issue. He just did the extra work and left her alone so she could process all that had just happened. It was well past nighttime and into early morning when the burying was finally over. Leadfoot decided it was better for both of them to move along the train track as planned earlier. There was no reason to stay here. Elizabeth got up with Leadfoot's help and started walking with him along the track. They weren't moving fast but that was okay. As long as they were moving. Neither spoke for a few hours. They stopped at a vacated campsite that was near a river. Elizabeth went down to the river to wash off and try to refresh herself while Leadfoot heated up the rest of their food and a little of the food that he'd taken off the dead men. He'd also taken their weapons and the slender man's shoes. But he didn't tell Elizabeth that. Not just yet.

"So where are we?" Elizabeth asked as she got up from sleeping on the floor of yet another boxcar. She had a sore neck last night when she fell asleep and still had it when she woke up this morning. Leadfoot didn't answer her. He just stared out at the mountains. The last few days were non-eventful. They had been lucky to catch a friendly train. That is, a train with an engineer that didn't mind turning his head the other direction when they hopped into an empty boxcar. Of course, it also helped that Leadfoot "greased" the engineer with a little cash to allow it to happen. The first few hours were always a little sketchy because one never knew if the engineer would keep his side of the deal or not. This time they were lucky. Not only did they find a safe train to be on, but they also found a long traveling train. It only stopped in a few "tank towns" for a mere few minutes and then they were off. After what Elizabeth had been through, it was nice for both of them to just stare out the opening of the boxcar at the scenery as it flew by. What beautiful scenery they saw. For the last couple of days, Elizabeth got to see mountains for the first time as they finished traveling through New York and then on to Pennsylvania.

Leadfoot softly spoke to himself, "Everyone should see the beautiful sunrises as the sun comes up from behind the mountains.

It's good for the soul." Elizabeth heard him and she agreed as she gazed at the wild wonder of the Appalachian Mountains.

"I've never known of such beauty. The bright yellow sun slowly rising behind the mountains makes them different hues of blue. Absolutely magnificent!" It was Leadfoot's turn to agree with her. "What's your favorite, Leadfoot, sunrises or sunsets?"

He thought for a moment, "Well, the way I see it is that sunrises give promises of a new start to each and every day. They also can erase problems that the night before has covered in darkness. As for sunsets, well, they can calm the chaos from your day and slow your mind down and allow you to be thankful for the opportunity of life for the next day." He watched her after he spoke to see her reaction hoping that he could gauge her emotions from killing that guy a few days ago. No luck. He was starting to wonder if maybe she was a little tougher than he thought.

The train was slowing to a stop to fill up one of the tankers with water. This stop was next to an apple orchard with the season's first batch of apples starting to ripen. So, they quickly jumped off to grab a couple. Neither of them really minded the tartness since it was a tad early in the season for the apples. Wild blackberries were always found along the train track. They grabbed a handful of them as they walked back to their railcar. Both of them were okay with the fruit since it was going to be their diet for the next couple of days.

After they snacked on apples and berries, Leadfoot wanted to teach her some of the aspects of the hobo life. Later that day, the next stop the train made was at a small town in West Virginia. The train was to pick up coal and fill up a few of the hopper cars that the engine was pulling. Leadfoot took it upon himself to snatch a few of the smaller pieces of the coal that had spilled off the side of one of the hoppers to the ground. He told Elizabeth that if she had planned on being in this way of life for a while, then this was a good time for her to learn a little bit more of the hobo symbols that she would see along the tracks. He used the coal to draw different symbols on the side of an old wooden box. Some of the symbols stood for phrases like "a kind lady lives here" or "food available for work." A couple others stood for a "dishonest man" or "policeman lives here." There were many other symbols that she would have to learn. Leadfoot reminded her that just because summertime was here didn't mean that "you couldn't do a little learnin'."

Since Leadfoot never answered Elizabeth's earlier question as to where they were, she asked him once again. Leadfoot was curious as to why she kept asking him that. It was hard for him to understand, but he needed to remember that she had never before left Boston. Her whole life was always bumping shoulders with strange people in a noisy atmosphere of constant commotion. She never had much time to be alone in a quiet place. He had to remember that he was showing her a whole new world. A world that he had taken for granted for all these years. "I believe we're somewhere in East Central Ohio right now. The tracks seem to be getting straighter and the land a little flatter. The mountains are turning into hills."

"How much longer are we going to stay on this train?"

"I don't know," he answered as he sneaked a glance at her direction. "I was going to let you decide what we were going to do." She just laid on her stomach with her chin propped up by her flattened hands staring out of the boxcar at the passing scenery.

Leadfoot couldn't wait any longer. He felt that they had to talk to Elizabeth about what had happened to the two men a few days ago. At the very least, try to get a sense of what she thought. Since that terrible night, all she really had been doing was sleeping and had been so quiet.

"I remember a time when I first started hitting the rails," he said. "I had just dropped into a campsite or hobo jungle, I should say. There was a sort of nervous tension in the air. People were all outta sorts. Like, I don't know, as if they were all trying to continue a conversation after it was interrupted, know what I mean?"

Elizabeth acknowledged him by turning her head and looking towards him. Never lifting her chin off her folded hands.

"I debated staying there," he continued, "but I was dead dog tired since I had walked all day long and just thought I'd get a few hours of shut eye before I'd go back to padding the hooves at dawn. After a few minutes of listening to the nervous talk, I realized that a guy showed up at the hobo jungle brandishing a bat and was swinging it like he was Billy O'Brien of the Washington Senators. They said that the bat wielder was talking all kinds of gibberish. He quite possibly was a canned heater, uh . . . um, well, that means he drank a potentially deadly mixture of homemade rotten grain alcohol and water . . . anyway back to the story. Apparently, guys were diving to the ground so to miss the mammoth swings. But one poor soul didn't drop quick enough and had his jawbone displaced a few feet from where he was sitting. Now I don't really know what happened to the wanna-be-home-run-hitter, but a part of that jawbone was still lying there in the grass. I saw it with my own peepers. That's when I decided to go it alone and leave. I was goin' to take my chances out there alone in case that guy came back to the camp. So, I found some tall grass and laid down and used the moon as my blanket that night."

"I know what you're getting at, Leadfoot," Elizabeth interrupted with her head still laying on her folded hands. "You're using that story to help me relate to what happened the other day. You're trying to figure a way to ask me how killing that man is affecting me. So just ask me. No need for a long drawn out – "

"I'm concerned about you, Elizabeth." It was his turn to interrupt. "I understand that your quietness and sleepiness pertain to that awful event. But how do you feel?"

Elizabeth thought for a moment or two. She felt that it was time for her to open up to Leadfoot a little bit about her life. She had been thinking about this for the last few days as she stared out of the railcar. She was kind of scared about what he would think of her.

Would he judge her?

Judge her for who she was?

Or even worse, judge her for who she is?

"I didn't have very good role models in Boston," she began. Leadfoot had been leaning against the railcar door, but he sat down crossed-legged on the floor near her as she started talking. "There were good people that lived in my neighborhood as well as in my tenement. But they always seemed to be moving away after a short while. I don't know if it was because of the poor living conditions or what. What seemed to be the mainstay in my environment was the dirty low lifes, hustlers, muggers, grifters, swindlers, thugs, and hoodlums. Add in a lot of dirty, smelly poor immigrants that would do whatever it was to get a leg up on one another. That was my living standard, my norm. With every person that was joyful, there were five trying to con that joy from each other for a price."

"I don't know where my dad is," she continued. "I'm not sure he is even alive. The last time I saw him he was bouncing down the make-shift fire escape to evade having to pay a gambling debt. My mom is dead. Dead by the hands of a vile Russian immigrant. I believe she was killed because my father owed him a large amount of gambling debts."

"The Russian's name was Nikita." Elizabeth shuddered from just saying his name. "He chased after me and surely would have killed me after he had his way with me. But I fought back. I eventually escaped from him, but in the process saw him kill a few others. I had to act quickly and decided to jump on a train that was literally leaving town just then. It wouldn't take a genius to look into my future and see how my life would have turned out if I had stayed in that environment. So, with that, as I see it, I have no family left." Leadfoot simply stared at her, soaking in every word that came from her lips. He didn't want to interrupt her. He was afraid that if he did, she would clam up and not continue with her story. He was getting a close look into this girl's being. She had seen and done more things than he had expected.

"I'm okay with taking that man's life. What concerns me about it is how easily and quickly it came to me. I don't know if I had some pent-up emotion from dealing with Nikita or what. But it was going to be him or me. If you remember, I told him I was going to kill him and I kept my word. I guess he'll never realize that I kept it." She paused for a couple moments then continued. "I think the death of those two men will always live in my head. But it had to be done. Better them than us. I just need to do what I can to keep on living."

It seemed to Leadfoot that she was still struggling to validate her actions. He thought he should encourage and help her along with talking it out. "So, do you think that from now on you don't need to worry about dying, but simply worry about how you'll live your life?"

Elizabeth thought back to the few moments after the slender man had died and how she thought he was lucky for not having to fight for his life anymore.

"I don't know," she finally said, "but with what I recently experienced, I'm starting to wonder if living hurts more than dying."

The train had taken them through some beautiful scenery for the past couple of days. The layout of the land had gone from the mountains of Pennsylvania and West Virginia to the hills and flat lands of Ohio. The two had decided to stay on the "friendly" train until they got completely out of the hills. "Walking up and down the hills will numb our hooves if we get off now," Leadfoot had said earlier when they were deciding on what to do. The train was going to Chicago, Illinois. First, it had to make a stop in Ft Wayne, Indiana and drop off a couple passenger cars that had to be sent south to make a stop in an up-and-coming town called Harrisburg in Indiana. This town was becoming a popular destination for people and businesses since there was a discovery of an abundant amount of natural gas, one of the biggest discoveries of natural gas in the country. So plentiful that many companies had planned on moving their factories there with the promise of free natural gas.

The day ended with another beautiful sunset followed by a magnificent starry night. A cool breeze flowing through the moving railcar and the repetitive noise and motion made a peaceful sleep come quickly for the two.

The next day was going to be hot. It was already muggy just after sunrise. Elizabeth woke up to see Leadfoot leaning against the open railcar door. She got up and moseyed over to him. The train was passing alongside a river. Every once in a while, you could see a tuft of smoke coming from what Elizabeth thought to be campfires.

"There's a lot more cook fires here than usual," Leadfoot said.

"Why is that? And how do you know?"

"It seems to me that the last time I was in this area there wasn't much happening. There was just one rail line through here. It looks like there are more rail lines now," he said to himself more than speaking to her. He leaned his head out a little bit to get a better look as to why the train was slowing down a little bit. "Whoa, look up the line there! What the heck? There's a train bridge! That's new!"

Elizabeth leaned out a little bit under Leadfoot's pointed finger. She was feeding off his excitement now. The train slowed down a little bit more as it came to the bridge. Slowly rails left the earth and reached over the river. Leadfoot was an overgrown kid. He quickly sat down on the edge of the rail car with his legs extending out. He held out his arms like he was flying. They were at least forty feet over the water. Then the flight was over, and they were back on solid ground.

"Boy! Was that ever exhilarating," Leadfoot said with a cheesy smile stretching from ear to ear. "I bet that's about as close to flying as a person could ever get. I've been on other bridges before, but this one is new. I wasn't expecting it to be here."

As they crossed over the river there was a beautiful big sign that simply said, Welcome to Our Town. "This place seems friendly enough," Elizabeth mused. The train whistled a couple of more times as it came closer to the edge of town. After a few moments, it shuddered and screeched to a stop. She looked over at Leadfoot and reminded him about their agreement about getting off the train this morning. And that's exactly what they did. They climbed out of the railcar and Elizabeth looked back at it. She was going to miss that railcar. She had really needed that temporary safe place for the last few days. But she was now excited to see what this day was going to bring her way. She looked around for Leadfoot, but he was gone. For a moment she started to panic. She found him already walking away from the train in a hurry. She had forgotten that it wasn't wise to be hanging around the train cars. So, she grabbed her bindle stick and went after him.

"Okay," Leadfoot started, "You need to look around for a symbol. A marking that another hobo may have left for others to give us an idea about this town. Remember some of the symbols we discussed the other day?" Elizabeth remembered. She started looking on the nearest trees with no luck. There weren't any buildings or structures within a half mile or so from them. Then she remembered the welcome sign. She ran back to it.

"Look over here, Leadfoot," she yelled with excitement. She had found something. He had already started walking over to her when she had yelled for him. When he got there, she was pointing at the backside of the post, and this is what she found:

Leadfoot was really proud of her for finding this. "Okay. You found a marking. Now. What does it mean? It doesn't really mean anything unless you know what it stands for."

Now it was Elizabeth's turn to wear the cheesy smile. "It means that there is food here if you work." Leadfoot frowned and crossed his arms and then tapped a finger to his chin. He was in deep thought and trying to decide if she was right or not. "Don't even try to act like I'm wrong, Leadfoot, I know I'm right." He couldn't hold back his smile any longer and gave her a tussle of her chopped hair.

"It's rather early in the morning and I'm hungry. These two apples aren't going to hold us all day. I say we go into town and see what kinda work there is for a couple of hobos." So off through the knee-high weeds they went.

Elizabeth had expected that they would walk down the hardened dirt road that led to the edge of town. But instead, Leadfoot led her towards the campfires. "Why are we going this way?" She asked. "Wouldn't the food and work be in town?"

"Absolutely, but we need to get the layout of the town. Just because the marking that you found suggested that we should be able to find friendly people to provide food for work doesn't mean everyone in town is friendly and honest. There are a lot of people that will take advantage of us for a hard day of work. So, the best way to find good work is to go to the ones that are receiving it."

"The hobos at the campsites," Elizabeth surmised. Leadfoot gave her an affirming nod and corrected her by reminding her that they were called hobo jungles not campsites. Calling them campsites implied that people stayed for just a day. The truth was that the people may leave from time to time, but the materials stayed behind.

The smell of the smoldering smoke floating from the cook fires earlier in the morning led them to the hobo jungle. They came upon the first area and found no one there. The only thing there was a pallet that was used to sleep on and soggy burnt wood and ashes that recently cooked someone's breakfast. Elizabeth scanned over the other spots in the hobo jungle. There were a lot of make-shift shanties made from old wooden boards and scrap metal indicating that this place had been established here for a while. Some of them had half broken bricks used as flooring or to help hold wall materials in place. Other places were simple grassy areas beaten down by someone sleeping there through the night. She was also surprised at how tidy the places were. One would think that these types of places were trashy and junky. They surprisingly were not.

"This is a good sign, Tumbleweed. Most hobo jungles that I've been to don't have sturdy sleeping and cooking areas. That tells me that there is plenty simple work to be had and people have spent a lotta time here."

"Leadfoot, I've noticed that there are tin cans resting on logs at the last two fire sites. They are all turned upside down. Is that symbolic or some type of sign?"

Leadfoot showed his stained teeth as he smiled. "No, that has no significance whatsoever. They are turned upside down so rainwater won't get in them and rust them out. We cook with the empty cans when there aren't any pots or pans readily available. It's impossible to carry a bunch of stuff with you. So, most of the stuff is just left for the next person to use."

"This here pot in my hand is good . . . good for goose eggs and it'll put a goose egg on your noggin if you's come any closer to my bedroll. Now git!" The threat came from an average sized person a couple campfires away from them. The hobo was waving the pot at them.

"Whoa, whoa, friend take it easy," said Leadfoot. He took off his hat and stuck his hands out to show that they weren't hostile. On the other hand, Elizabeth placed her hand on the end of her bindle stick. Ever so ready to pop the end off and expose the blade. "All we want is a little information. We're just looking for any particulars on the lay of the land. Specifically, if the work environment is friendly or not, that's all."

The pot swinging hobo didn't care. "Git, I tell ya! Git! You's ain't gonna find anything of value here, unless you value a pot knot big enough for a calf to suckle on. Now git! GIT, GIT, GIT!"

Another hobo had just walked back from the river and entered the jungle carrying a canteen of water. "Hey now, leave those two alone," he said as he pointed to Leadfoot and Elizabeth. "I don't know the young one, but that big guy is the world renown Leadfoot Frankie. He's the nicest, kindest guy on the rails as long as you don't provoke him. Why, I've seen him kindly shake a man's hand and then rip it off and smack the man in the face with it because the guy tried to slip his other hand into Leadfoot's back pocket."

Leadfoot's face pinched all together in thought as to who this guy was until that last part was said. Then a big smile came on his face, "Holy Toledo! It's been many moons since I saw you. And that guy deserved it. That was Grandaddy's watch he was trying to jack roll from me. It wasn't in my back pocket. It was my vest pocket. I woulda never let him reach that far behind me." They laughed as they shook hands.

Elizabeth kept her eyes on the pot wielding hobo. "So, you really pulled off that man's hand and slapped him with it?" Both guys looked over at her and laughed even louder. She made a mental note that neither man actually answered her question.

"I'm sorry," Leadfoot said, "I should introduce you two. Tumbleweed, this here is Toledo Teddy, an old friend of mine. He hops a bobtail that runs from Toledo to Columbus in this great state of Ohio. Toledo, this here is Tumbleweed. I met up with her back east a while ago. Trying to teach her the way of hobohemia while she's doin' what she's doin'."

"It's a pleasure to meet your acquaintance…Tumbleweed, was it?" He shook her hand and stared into her eyes. He thought something was amiss. "I suppose you explained to her that living this life is a dangerous one. Especially for a female."

She quickly pulled her hand away from him and started to say something when Leadfoot spoke up before she did, "Yes, yes. She's learning as she goes. Tumbleweed here, should we say, is learning on the job. Learning by the seat of her pants."

"Well, I hope she doesn't lose the seat of her pants." He had genuine concern in his voice.

"Thanks for your worry," a perturbed Tumbleweed said. "But I think I'm doing pretty good so far. Why, just a couple of days ago these two guys . . ."

"Speaking of learning on the job," Leadfoot interrupted by changing the subject. He made a mental note to tell Elizabeth to keep her trap shut about past situations. Especially situations that dealt with the loss of life. Some people in this life hear others talk about killing and see it as boastfulness. Most times it comes back to haunt the ones that are thought to be showing off. "This town seems to be growing. That railroad bridge is new. The added rail lines show promise of things to come. And the great Toledo Teddy is here. So, what gives?"

The pot waving hobo had gone back to his own business. He must have thought that Toledo Teddy had things under control. "Don't mind that ole antique," Teddy said. "He's this hobo jungle's kitchen mechanic. He's a little paranoid, that's all."

"Kitchen mechanic?" Elizabeth wasn't sure she understood.

"Yeah, you know crumb boss, camp cook. He's the one that fixes the stew and such when there are a lot of us here. That's how he earns his keep in the jungle. We bring him scraps of 'gredients and he builds our meals with them."

Elizabeth rolled her eyes. She ignored the cook and then set all her attention to sizing up ole Teddy. She pointed her bindle stick at him but spoke to Leadfoot. "What's the big deal about him being here? A lot of guys are here. Why is he so important?" Teddy was getting mildly perturbed at her. So was Leadfoot.

To calm things down a little bit, Leadfoot thought he'd educate her on some things about Teddy. "Teddy is a big deal in this area. He is an important man for people like us. He's what we call a middleman. Teddy is from up north in Ohio and rides a bobtail, like I said earlier, from Toledo to Columbus. A bobtail is a local freight train that doesn't travel far because it pulls just a few cars. So as a middleman, if there are jobs that us hobos, trustworthy hobos, can do, Teddy gets connected with the craftspeople and supplies them with their biggest need . . . us." Leadfoot turned his attention to Teddy. "So, as I was saying earlier, things seem rather prosperous around here. Tumbleweed and I hopped off here after spending a couple days riding the rails. We thought that we'd stretch our legs a bit and meander on into town. Maybe we'd find something to eat. We're more than willing to work for our keep. Do you think you could point us in the right direction?"

"Wanna do some earnin' of your keep, huh?" Teddy pointed his chin towards Elizabeth, "Suppose she could do manual labor? Her jaw seems that it could work up a good sweat from all that mouthin'."

Elizabeth knew that he was antagonizing her, and she ignored his tone. "Leadfoot has been teaching me that the code for the road of hobos means that the only things you should take are the things that someone gives you in good faith, things that you've earned through hard work and things that the good Lord provides for us." She held out her bindle stick and weapon. "I've been given these from a new friend a while ago along with food and shelter. Lord knows that He has provided us with fruit to eat from the land on our recent journey. We're ready to work these bones and muscles to earn some hot food and a place to sleep. We're not bums or tramps, we're hobos."

"Woo hoo, Leadfoot, you got yourself a handful with this one," Toledo Teddy teased. "She knows how to ruffle feathers, mightily, and then knows how to smooth them over before they can get tousled again." Leadfoot silently agreed. So did Elizabeth.

"Well, let me think about what jobs there are to be taken," Teddy rubbed his bristly chin in thought for a moment and then snapped his finger. "Leadfoot, I'd say there are quite a few jobs that would suit you both. I'm just thinking about which pusher is more accepting towards our kind," Teddy looked over to Elizabeth. "A pusher is a man in charge of a certain job. I presume you're not a bohunk or a flannel mouth are ya, youngin'?"

"I don't know what those mean. I'm from Boston."

Teddy explained, "Well, a bohunk is a Polish person. A flannel mouth is Irish. I don't know exactly what or how that came upon them. That's just what I know they're called. I'm asking because there is a cousin Jack, or uh, I mean, an Englishman, that is a pusher on this here side of town. Just on the edge of town, he's building a school. He and his crew have taken kindly to the hobos. I guess it's because they are doing the menial jobs for only food or for a few coins. There's another cousin Jack that's turning the dirt roads into beautiful brick roads if that's something you're interested in. He hires mainly flannel mouths, I guess he likes bossing them around, but he also selects some traveling men from time to time. If I was you two that's where I'd start. Leadfoot, I'd venture a guess that you would like to be tallied into that knowledge box project, eh. Being that is your past expertise and all." Leadfoot ignored that statement by thanking him and ushering Elizabeth away from the hobo jungle. "I'll make sure that there is an area for you guys around the fire tonight and a place to rest your brain box. Oh! By the way, whatever you do, stay away from the two clothing factories north of town by the river. They are infested with candle eaters. Those guys come here and immediately get pushed up that way. The rotten lot that they are."

Leadfoot pinched his brows together in concern. "Are there a lot of candle eaters in this area?"

"Enough of them scoundrels to make you want to stay out of the way. They even have taken over one of the saloons in the middle of town. Ugh. Rascals. They give us people a bad name. There is always a bunch of them heading westward to work on the railroad and a few of them are always falling off the trains and ending up here for a while."

"Thanks for the information, Toledo. Hopefully we'll be back later. Let's go, Tumbleweed. Let's see if we can earn us enough for tonight before it gets too much hotter out here."

"So, who are the candle eaters Toledo Teddy was talking about? They sound like a rather unpleasant batch of folks."

Leadfoot Frankie tried to look impassive to her question, but Elizabeth saw right through his guise. He blew out a deep breath and said, "Russians."

Elizabeth tried to hold back her fear. The thought of possibly bumping into Nikita made her lose her breath and her knees weakened. She tried to act nonchalant about his answer, but Leadfoot could see her grip her bindle stick a little tighter in response.

8

They made it to town just as everyone was starting to work. Teams of horses were being driven to different job sites. They were pulling wagons of supplies that consisted of every variety of building materials that one could imagine. There were mules being used and even men were carrying materials after they were finished in the stockyards and unloading the never-ending trains that seemed to be coming to the town. Different languages were being spoken all through the area. It made you wonder how everyone could understand what was going on and being said. All the commotion going on made Elizabeth think of home back in Boston.

Leadfoot and Elizabeth asked around to see who was in charge of the different types of jobs. It didn't take long to find out. The hobos that were working seemed to be genuinely happy in helping them out. Based on what Teddy had said earlier about Leadfoot, Elizabeth presumed that they would be walking over to the schoolhouse project. Instead, he led them to the main guy who was in charge of laying bricks for the new roads in the downtown area. The two walked up to the man that was writing a list of materials on a flat piece of slate and then drawing lines to a list of names. He was already sweating profusely, and the stub of his cigar was no longer lit. But he kept grinding away at it with his bicuspids chewing it to shreds.

"Excuse me sir, we were told that you're the job pusher for the road of bricks. We'd like to help out for a few days if you could use us. We don't ask for much pay. Just a couple of coins and some daily food would suffice."

The man studied both of them as his anxiety was noticeably high by evidence of his gnawed cigar. "Deal!" He growled as he jabbed the cigar in their direction. "Have any experience with bricks? Not much is needed, actually. Just some muscle to move materials and common sense in stacking the bricks and aligning them into the sand base. I think even two hobos can figure that out."

"We have a lot of experience in a lot of stuff." Elizabeth lied. "Why, Leadfoot here built one of the best buildings . . ."

"Sir," Leadfoot interrupted Elizabeth once again, "how will we get paid for our work?"

"Give me your names or monikers, whatever you prefer, and I'll mark them down on this slate. At the end of the day, you'll be given a ticket. Good for a meal from that saloon across that street. No other saloon but that one. Drinking water for you will be from the troughs marked 'prisoners.'"

"Prisoners, sir? But we're not prisoners," Elizabeth remarked with concern on her face after the two had given him their monikers.

The stressed pusher was getting aggravated. He wanted this conversation finished. It had gone on long enough. "Yes, yes, yes, I know, I know," as he flailed his hands in the air, "we've been using prisoners from a local prison to help get these projects done because we're running way behind! But for cripes sake, they kept running away. I can't pay anymore guards and I don't have time to babysit those lags and yardbirds. We started shooting at them, but we were just wasting ammo. At least you hobos stay to work and don't need guards. Those lags wanted freedom. Your kind just wants food." He pointed at Leadfoot, "I can use you now! Grab that full wheelbarrow and follow me! You, young man," he said as he pointed the well chewed cigar at Elizabeth, Leadfoot prayed that she wouldn't correct him, "you grab those rakes and follow me too!" He turned and without waiting started to walk away from them. He grabbed his shredded cigar and threw it to the ground. He reached inside his shirt pocket and pulled out three more, selected one, and put the other two back in. He bit off the cap of the cigar and lit it. All of this without missing a step or bumping into anyone.

Leadfoot and Elizabeth got to work. The sun had reached its highest point for the day and kept launching its sun rays down on the back of their sticky sunburned necks. Elizabeth was glad to have this job. One where she was going to make a return on her effort. She felt like she had been penned up every day that she was in the railcar. This was something new and exciting for her. She felt like she had a purpose to wake up every morning no matter how maligned this job was to be. They had gotten to the work site and saw a huge heaping mound of bricks. The man that was to be in charge of them gave them the job of stacking bricks on pallets from that heaping mound. At first Elizabeth thought the job was easy until she realized that the bricks felt heavier and heavier as the day wore on. Her fingers and wrists ached as did her back from constantly bending over. She would watch Leadfoot and noticed that he didn't seem to have eagerness about the job like she did. She wondered if he decided on this job because he thought that it would be easier for her to handle. Who knows what job they could have taken at the school site. Maybe a more important job than what they were doing. She wondered why Leadfoot decided to work here instead of at the schoolhouse build.

"Leadfoot, I'm curious," she said as she reached for a few bricks to stack on her assigned pallet, "why didn't we go to the schoolhouse being built?"

"Because I didn't want to," was the short reply.

She continued as she reached for another handful of bricks and stacked them five bricks tall, "I mean . . . listening to Toledo Teddy, he made it sound that you were an expert brick mason and that the job was right for the picking for you. Did you think this was an easier job for me and that I couldn't do whatever it took to build a school?"

"I didn't want to." His answer was more terse this time. "We would still be stacking and loading bricks if we were over there." He followed his comment with an irritated wave towards the school site. It was one of those waves that looked like he was swatting at a fly with intent to kill it.

"That's quite possible for me, but I'm sure that you would have had a much more important job than this one. You would have gotten a job that would have been more suited than this crummy one."

Leadfoot was hot and getting tired, and frankly, he was a little out of shape. All this bending over was making him outright surly. "Enough with questions, Tumbleweed!!" He huffed. "I didn't want to! There's not an answer to every question you have!" He huffed some more. "Sometimes things are just what they are!"

Elizabeth was taken aback by his abruptness. "I just thought that we could have worked over there if you wanted to."

"If you want to go work over there, then go!!" He slammed a brick on a rock that was sticking out of the ground. The brick shattered like glass. Everyone stopped what they were doing and looked over at the commotion. Leadfoot, embarrassed by his actions, walked over to the trough marked for prisoners, picked up the metal dipper and took a long and much needed drink and then slammed the dipper on the ground. "Not everything is always about you. I didn't pick this job for you; I picked this job for me!"

Elizabeth stopped and stared at Leadfoot. She thought she may have prodded a might too much. "Get back to stacking those bricks, tenderfoot," someone yelled to Elizabeth. So, she did. And, of course, with an attitude.

After Leadfoot had had some time to cool off, he went back to work. He felt bad that he snapped at Elizabeth and tried to apologize to her, but she ignored him as if he was a stranger for the rest of the day. She was mad.

All she wanted to know was why.

That's all.

What harm was there.

They finished their workday and received a red ticket that was good for one meal at the saloon. Elizabeth didn't wait for Leadfoot. She kept her head down and followed the other hobos to the saloon. Inside the saloon was a free food counter full of salted meats. They were not allowed to eat from that counter. That counter was for paying customers. The idea was that they would come in and eat the free salted meat and then buy beer and whiskey to wash it down. What a marketing idea!

The hobos were instructed to not eat inside the establishment. They were to go around to the back and wait for their food. Tonight's meal was fried potatoes, onions, radishes, and sausage. Also added were two carrots and an apple and all the milk or water one could drink. Elizabeth traded her apple with another hobo for an extra carrot. She grabbed her meal and sat off in a tight circle of logs with other workers. She made sure there was no room for Leadfoot.

After she ate, she walked back to the hobo jungle by herself. She went over to the camp cook and gave him the extra carrot she had traded for. Teddy was good to his word. He had secured her and Leadfoot a place within the jungle. Not the best place, but, hey, it was her first night. Even in the hobo jungle one had to earn their way.

She waited until darkness and went to the river with her bindle stick for protection and jumped in. The slight chill of the water soothed her aching muscles from a hard day's work. She changed into other clothes and washed the dirt from the ones she had worn that day. She went back to the place that was provided for her to sleep and Leadfoot was there. She could hear him snoring way before she got there. There was an old yellow blanket waiting for her. She remembered it from Leadfoot's bindle. He had apparently left it for her as a sort of peace offering. She took it and went and laid under a tree clearly away from him.

This went on for the next week or so. Elizabeth didn't necessarily ignore him. She acknowledged him but rather avoided him.

She felt power in it. As inexperienced as she was in this way of life, this was a way for her to accumulate some needed self-power. She wondered if she could do this on her own without anyone's help. Leadfoot sensed what she was doing and he let it happen.

Saturday usually meant that the weekend was here. But they were so busy building the downtown roads that it might as well have been a Wednesday. The workers did get good news though. They were told that if they worked hard enough, they would be given Sunday off since it was a day of worship. Of course, no work also meant no food was to be provided for that day. They worked hard all day long and when the work was done, they raced to the saloon to eat just as hard.

Elizabeth finished eating and again she didn't wait for Leadfoot. She began following a couple of hobos back to the river area when she heard a bunch of singing and yelling coming from the direction of town. It was coming from a saloon in the middle of town. She debated for a moment and decided to walk over to the sound of the noises. It wasn't too dark yet. Maybe just dark enough for her to be able to get close without anyone noticing that she was too young to be there. She walked the two blocks and saw a large oak tree that was across the street from the saloon. She decided that that would be a good place to hide and snoop.

The outside of the saloon was rather dark, but when the front door opened, light came spilling out and she could see people shoulder to shoulder. Big burly people singing their hearts out. The singing sounded somewhat familiar to her even though it was a different language. The voices were hard and heavy. This must be the saloon that Teddy had warned about. The one the Russian people had taken over for their own.

She started wondering whether the idea of her being here alone was a wise one. She had a sinking feeling in the pit of her stomach. What if . . . what if she knew someone here in the saloon? No, there's no way she would know anyone. There's no way Nikita could be in there. Could he? Just as she was thinking all of this, the door of the saloon exploded outwardly. A man flew through the air with his arms flailing as his face and stomach landed on the boardwalk with a thud. Out walked two heavily bearded men. One of them held the fallen man up as the other one pounded the life out of him. Literally. The fallen man's lifeless body was dropped to the ground.

The two men spoke drunken Russian to each other as they scanned the area for any witnesses. Elizabeth closed her eyes and melted into the tree hoping not to have been seen. Now she knew it was a bad idea to be here but how could she leave without being spotted? She opened her eyes hoping that that was her only movement. She saw one of the men pointing in her direction. They both got up from the dead man and peered over that way. They stepped off the boardwalk and into the street in her direction. From behind her she smelled and felt the heavy breath and words spoken to her in thickened English, "What are you doing here? Do you think you have seen enough?"

Nikita.

Or so she thought.

She wasn't sure. She thought that if she looked down, she would be able to see her heart beating through her shirt. She started to slowly reach for the cleaver then realized that she had lost the element of surprise. Her bindle stick could be an option, but she decided that the best thing to do was to simply . . . cough. Cough real loud and shake the small bush that was in front of her.

The two Russians heard her from the street and saw the bush move. They started running towards her. She dropped to the ground exposing the man behind her. Just as the two men reached the tree she crawled through some taller bushes and got to the other side of the block. The three Russians began arguing and then another fight started. She wanted to see what was happening, but realized it was not safe.

Once the fight was in full swing, she stood up and ran back to the hobo jungle. She did slow down for a moment to see if anyone was following her. No one was from what she could tell. She saw the man whom she thought was Nikita and he was clearly out matched by the other two. She made it back to the hobo jungle knowing that she had witnessed the first man's murder. She wondered if she had watched yet another.

Sunday awarded the early morning with a cool breeze that made the hot air much more bearable. The antique camp cook had made enough biscuits with butter for the whole jungle. Leadfoot devoured both of his biscuits, but Elizabeth ate half of one and saved the rest for later. She grabbed her bindle stick and walked down to the edge of the river. She sat on a big rock and looked up into the sky. There were not many clouds out today. Those that were there would soon be burned off by the sun.

"Hey there, Tumbleweed," shouted Toledo Teddy as he climbed down to the riverbank, "You's not planning on making a hole in that water, are you?" He had to crawl over a couple of fallen trees to make the final ten feet to reach her.

"Make a hole in the water? What is that code for?" Sarcasm oozed out of her mouth.

"Aww, it's just hobo talk for suicide by drowning. You're not planning to, right?"

Elizabeth spun around to face Teddy, "What?! Lord, no. I'm likely to make a hole in the water with someone else besides me."

"Oh, I bet you would. You are probably the most sinister person to ever walk through this neck of the woods. Why, I'm surprised you haven't claimed the best spot in this here jungle by force for yourself."

"Hush." She looked over her shoulder and then leaned in towards him. "You've stumbled upon my sinister plan. Back out slowly while you have the chance." They both laughed at the thought of it. She thought he laughed too much. Way too much. Almost as if it was faked. Maybe to hide a bit of nervousness?

"Wow. I'd recognize that blaring laugh from any jungle," came a voice from the trees. It was Leadfoot. He was high stepping the tall grass and climbing over the downed trees. He was carrying a flexible stick that he was going to use for a makeshift fishing pole. He thought that Teddy was alone down there. Then he saw Elizabeth and stopped mid step. "Is it okay if I fish here? I hope I'm not interrupting anything. It's a good spot with those trees leaning over the river here. Kinda shady for me and the fish."

"Suit yourself. It's a free country," Elizabeth had turned her back and attention towards the sky.

Teddy began to feel uncomfortable. "Well, I best be going. I might go see what the ole antique has in store for a late lunch. He muttered something about making vegetable soup with all the vegetables he's been getting." Teddy eased along into an atmosphere that was less foreboding.

Leadfoot took out one of his daggers and quickly swiped a few small twigs off the makeshift fishing pole. He pulled a hook from his hat and tied it to some string that he had in his pocket. He produced a worm and in no time had the worm on the hook and the hook in the water. They both stared at the worm bobbing up and down, up and down. Elizabeth found it to be rather relaxing. After staring at the worm for a few minutes, Leadfoot thought that he'd slowly start up a conversation, though he knew he had to be careful. Tumbleweed had been rather temperamental as of late.

"This is one of my favorite things to do to pass the time. You are actually doing something, you have a goal, but in essence you are just relaxing." He gave the line a little twitch. "Have you ever fished?"

"No, I never understood the whole idea of it. You just sit on your butt and jiggle a worm on a line. It doesn't seem to be all that hard. Seems like a big waste of time if you ask me." She flipped over onto her stomach and folded her hands under her chin. She wished she had her long hair back so it would keep the sun off her sunburned neck. She was just about to doze off when she heard Leadfoot squeal. He had been sitting on the edge of the rock but was standing up and pulling at the string. Elizabeth was now standing up right next to him. She didn't even remember getting up during all the excitement. "Holy moly, you got one. I've never seen someone catch a fish!" Leadfoot slowly pulled the fish up on the rock. Elizabeth nervously watched it flop back and forth. She wasn't sure what to think about that.

"That's a white crappie. Not necessarily a big one, but big enough to fry up over a fire. Mighty good eatin'. Especially if we can get a few more." He looked around as if he was looking for something. "What do ya think? You wanna give it a try?" Just a few minutes ago Elizabeth didn't want anything to do with it or want anything to do with Leadfoot. Now she was intrigued.

"I-I-I don't know what to do. I don't have a worm. Do I have to use a worm?"

Leadfoot suggested for her to put a small piece of the biscuit from breakfast on the hook. "Now mash it on tight and be sure not to stab yourself with the hook. Flip the baited hook over there under that overhanging tree. Now you just wait." He grabbed his own bindle stick that was by the rock and began fixing some string and a nail to the end of it. He got out another hook and started to knot the hook on the line.

"Something is pulling on the hook! Something is pulling on the hook! Leadfoot, I think something is on the line!" She started to walk back, stepped off the rock and fell backwards pulling the rod and fish with her. The fish smacked her in the face with its tail and she let out a screech. Leadfoot went over to her.

"My, oh my, you got yourself a beaut. That's a catfish. It's a small one, but it's worth eatin' for sure." He helped her get the fish off the hook. She helped him find a few more worms and then back to the poles. She had caught the fishing fever and couldn't get enough. After about an hour, they had caught five fish. There wasn't much else to do that day and they had plenty of shade. They decided that they had enough fish. He showed her how to clean them and then they cooked them over a fire. A meal fit for a king. Elizabeth had never eaten fish that fresh. Come to think of it, she couldn't even remember the last time she had even eaten fish.

The fire was extinguished and the two of them sat under the shade tree listening to the river. About fifteen minutes had passed and neither one of them had said a word. Leadfoot thought that this was about the best time as any for him to apologize to her for his crossness the other day. He hoped that she would stay and listen to him. "You know, Tumbleweed, I'm sorry for being so irritable that day on the job. I hope you accept my apology."

She sat there watching the river. "You know, I was happy that day. It's weird. I've never had to work like that. I was going to earn my own way. I was tired and exhausted, but I was happy and excited. I didn't understand why you weren't in a good mood. I thought that this is what we do, you know, work for food and whatever. I expected that you would be just as happy. When I asked you those questions and you got short with me, it reminded me that I was just a dumb kid and that I really didn't know all that I thought that I did."

"You are far from dumb. You've been able to get out of situations that a lot of adults wouldn't know how. Listen, when you started asking me all those questions, I felt like I was being second guessed on my decision to work on the road and not the schoolhouse. I can't believe how frustrated it made me. I guess it just conjured up some memories that I really wanted to forget about."

"From your past?"

"Yeah. Way past. It's the reason I hit the rails." He looked out to the river. His eyes were focused on the water, but his mind was miles and miles away.

Elizabeth sat up. "So, tell me about those memories and why you decided to ride the rails."

"I don't know. I don't think you need to know about my past. You don't need to know everything about everything."

"So why is it okay for you to know about my past but I don't know anything about yours? Do you remember what you said to me when we first met? You told me to trust you. And I did. Now why can't you trust me? I think you should tell me. We're friends, aren't we? Why do you think your past is worse than mine, if that's what you think? Let me be the judge of that for myself. No two ways about it. It either is or isn't. Black or white."

"My, you just jump right into the fire. There's no beating around the bush for you is there? For your information, not everything is black and white. There are a thousand different shades of gray in life."

Elizabeth thought for a moment about what he said. "Maybe it's right for your life, but for me everything is black or white. The 'is' or the 'isn't.' There's less problems and mystery to deal with."

Leadfoot scooped up a pile of pebbles with one hand. Then he examined one of them and tossed it into the river. It seemed he was gathering his thoughts from each thrown rock. "At one time I was raised in southern Tennessee. I was an only child. My parents and I moved around a lot, living with extended family and such. But I called southern Tennessee home. The place was Barnett. I guess because most of the people that lived there had the last name of Barnett. There wasn't much in that little town. Just a Baptist church, general store, blacksmith, and a one room schoolhouse. We didn't even have a jail. No need for one. Practically everyone was family. Except for us. My pa was the minister at the Baptist church. One cold winter when I was about your age, Elizabeth, my ma took hold of a fever. A fever that she just couldn't break. In the end, it ended up breaking her."

He continued. "I'd seen my pa lead many funeral services in my time, but it was so unreal to watch him perform ma's funeral on the top of that mountain. It tore him up and eventually tore us up. He turned to the bottle on most nights. He was a mean drunk. I ended up doing most of the chores around the house while pa was recovering from a hangover or because he was too busy writing one of his fiery sermons. The schoolhouse was one room with twenty-two kids, ages six to fourteen. I was determined to finish school, though it was hard doing almost all the chores around the house and dealing with pa during the trouble times. One day in the early spring I came home to show pa the outstanding marks that I had received from the teacher, but he was not there. After many days of him not showing up I said something to the teacher about it. There was a group of men that went out searching for him. An empty whiskey bottle was found near my ma's grave, and it was determined that my pa slipped or fell off the side of the mountain. Most people believed that he jumped to his death. His body was never recovered. That happened in my last year of school."

He went on. "One of the things that I was really interested and excelled in was construction, particularly using formulas and logic to build things. I had received a couple books on building and construction, and I read them during my free time. I practically had them memorized. Coal had been discovered near our little town and people had started to move into our area. The one room schoolhouse simply couldn't hold all the kids. So, with a little help from my teacher and her husband, who owned the general store, we raised money that went to materials to build a bigger and better brick schoolhouse. Most of the local men donated their time for free to help with this project. Everything was going wonderful until we found out that our funds were getting low."

His story continued. "Two brothers whose last name was Barnett, imagine that, were finishing building our town's first bank. They were willing to donate the rest of their material, which was mainly brick and mortar. A little extra money was also given with the understanding that it had to be paid back in the future. The only problem in dealing with the Barnett brothers was that they wanted to take over the building process. They said to take it or leave it. So, for the good of the children, I allowed them to bully their way in. It didn't matter though because everyone knew that I was responsible for the project. One of the owners of the new coal mining companies had been watching the schoolhouse project and had told me to come find him after the schoolhouse was built. He wanted to offer me a job within his company designing one of the coal mines!"

Leadfoot went on. "After a few more weeks of building, the good ole knowledge box was built. The only concern that I had was that the Barnett brothers had skimped on some of the material and design plans. The wind seemed to always come from the west and there were a lot of trees on that side of the property, so I had reinforced the west wall with a huge fireplace. The brothers had removed that fireplace from the plans and decided to install a wood stove in the middle of the room to provide heat. They said that this was the 'in thing' and it would produce heat more evenly throughout the schoolhouse. I had also planned on naming the schoolhouse after my mom as her memorial. The Barnett brothers had changed that also and renamed it the Barnett School. It was finished and after a quick celebration, the new schoolhouse was put to use."

It was hard, but he continued. "Within the first week of using the school, a big storm came through town. It blew a big tree down on top of the schoolhouse and it crashed through the wall. It caved in that entire side of the building. If the Barnett brothers had kept to my plan, the big fireplace that I wanted installed would have been able to sustain the tree. But they didn't and so the wall didn't. Terrible news spread through the town that ten kids were killed along with the teacher. The townspeople were in an uproar and deservedly so. The Barnett brothers were able to convince the townspeople, which were practically all their kin, that my plans and I were responsible for the destruction. Quickly the whole town was against me. I tried to tell the people that it was unjust to blame me. My plans were flawless. But no one would listen to me. They would rather believe one of their own than an outsider with a lot of misfortune like me. I was an easy fall guy for that horrible event."

He explained some more. "Everyone had turned their back on me, even the owner of the general store whose wife had been the teacher. I had nowhere to turn. I walked down to the new coal mining company to talk with the owner that was going to offer me a job. News had gotten to him quicker than I could get to him. He ordered me off the property and to never come back. So, I went back to my small house totally dispirited and not knowing what to do. When I turned the corner at the end of town, I could see black smoke billowing from large orange flames engulfing what was left of my house. I ran as fast as my two lead feet would allow. My house was on fire. Arson! Someone had set my house on fire in retaliation for the school debacle. By the time I got there it was too far gone for me to put it out all by myself. All I could do was to stand there and mumble to myself that it wasn't my fault. It really wasn't my fault."

Leadfoot went on. "I had nowhere to go. It was getting late in the afternoon, and I was tired and hungry. I started to meander my way up the lane from my house back into town utterly dejected and trying to decide what to do. I walked up the dirt road towards the cemetery where my ma was buried. I needed to sit and think. A man older than me approached me and asked me if I was the dead preacher man's son. Now I've never seen this man before and didn't rightly know if I should trust him or not. I told him yes and he then asked if I was the one that everyone was going to grab and string me up in a tree for the schoolhouse fiasco. I didn't answer but the fear in my eyes told him exactly who I was."

Leadfoot quoted the man. "'Let's go! Let's go now! You need to get the lead out of your feet and move, Mister!' The words spewed out of the man's mouth like a rushing river. 'They gonna kill you dead. Here, follow me on this path through the trees. It'll lead to a stream. You will have to follow the stream which will eventually flow into the river in about an hour or so. Just before you get to the mouth of the river, there will be a cave with a good-lookin' guy in there waitin' for you at a campfire. And yes, I'm that good lookin' guy.' The man let out a cackling laugh. 'I'll have some vittles waiting for you. Now git the lead outta your feet and butt and be gone before your dirt nap is confirmed in the morning.'"

Elizabeth sat up straight, "That man was Papa Gio!!! I knew it when you said, 'a cackling laugh!' He helped you get out of town?"

"Yes. He had heard about the town and its growing pains while he was traveling up north from Georgia. He had gotten there just as a group of men had set fire to my house and had overheard them talking about stretching my neck. Anyway, I got to the cave early that evening and he was there waiting for me. I don't know how he beat me there, but he did. I slept in that cave that night. Before morning light came, we had left camp and walked the trails through the Appalachians. We found railroad tracks later on. He showed me how and when to ride the rails. The rest is history."

"Did you ever go back to that town?"

"Nope," sadly he spoke. "Never have."

"Not even to see your ma's grave?"

Leadfoot took a deep breath and slowly blew it out. "My ma isn't there. She's in sunrises and sunsets. I see her in the birds that fly along the racing trains through the plains. I see her reflection in the water's ripples when the wind blows just right. That's when I know she's here." Elizabeth now realized why he loved the sunsets and sunrises so much. She was jealous of the thought of loving someone like that and wondering if she'll ever feel that way about someone.

There was a commotion going on at the hobo jungle. Men started getting louder and louder. Leadfoot and Elizabeth jumped up from the edge of the river, climbed over the fallen tree and ran up the embankment. Just as they made it to the tree line at the edge of the jungle the camp cook, with a well-worn carpet bag in his hand, jumped out in front of the two of them and tried to force them both down onto the ground. Leadfoot went down. Elizabeth refused. The cook begged for her to get down out of sight.

"You need to get flatter than a flitter, Tumbleweed. There's some threatening candle eaters in camp. I'm not sure what they're here for, but they mean to do harm," said the cook in a very serious tone.

Leadfoot pulled Elizabeth down to the ground. She wasn't happy about the force he used but matters must be serious because the camp cook had fear in his eyes. This wasn't the time for her to be brash. Elizabeth thought that a couple of them looked familiar, but she wasn't sure why . . . then she remembered.

Leadfoot was concerned with what was going on. "So, what all do you know about what's going on, old timer?"

"I had just got the cookwares cleaned up and was thinking about doing a little fishin'. I heard about the big haul you guys got and I thought I'd try my luck. Next thing I knew those four Russians came crashing into the jungle. They started upsetting someone's bedding and then slung cooking utensils at anyone in sight. One of our guys took a frying pan to the chops and another was being roughed up by a couple of them darn candle eaters. They kept threatening to poke holes in people if any of us talked about the circumstances last night at their bar. Nobody seemed to know what in tarnation they were jawing about. I don't have much luck with those candle eaters. My experience with them amounts to pretty much whatever they threaten, they tend to follow through, whether it's a legit order or not. They feel like they have to keep up appearances as being the tough bunch. I don't want to be here when the earth opens up and hellfire rains from the clouds. So, with that . . . I'm outta here. Adios."

And just like that, the kitchen mechanic started padding the hoof towards the rail. He didn't even think about jumping onto a steam hog that was sitting there on the track. He would take his chances on down the rail. That's how bad he wanted away from there. Leadfoot and Elizabeth stayed right where they were until things calmed down a bit. After they finally did, the two got up and went to check on their belongings. The place was in disarray. Objects were strewn all over the place. The atmosphere was full of gloom and dejection from what had transpired earlier. As the two were claiming their possessions, Teddy walked swiftly up to Leadfoot and pulled him aside. They stood behind an oak tree. Teddy did most of the talking and he did most of the listening. Leadfoot called Elizabeth over to them.

"Elizabeth," he started, "there may be trouble coming this way. Teddy, here, tells me that there was a murder out front of the bar that the Russians have claimed as their own."

"I know," she interrupted, "I saw it." Teddy and Leadfoot exchanged a glance.

She could feel the tension in Teddy's voice and manner. "What did you see, Tumbleweed?"

Now Elizabeth was getting nervous. She felt like she was about to be in over her head. "Everything," she blurted out. "Everything. I just wanted to explore a little bit of the town. It wasn't dark yet. There was no harm in doing that."

Teddy interrupted, "Oh there was harm done . . . "

It was Leadfoot's turn to interrupt Teddy. "Shut up and let her talk!" Both Teddy and Elizabeth flinched at the sudden growling that came from Leadfoot. This made Elizabeth feel more weight pressing down on her. Leadfoot took a deep breath and calmly asked her to continue.

"I was just out walking and exploring a little around town. There weren't very many people around. I never felt unsafe. I heard a bunch of music and singing. I haven't heard that since I've been away from home. There was a small park across from that saloon that you're talking about. The next thing I knew I was witnessing two guys beating up another guy. I'm sure they killed him."

"They did." Teddy's current butting in on Elizabeth made Leadfoot grumble at him.

"The next thing I knew there was a man behind me asking me if i knew what I was doing there and if I had seen enough. I then made some noise, enough noise for the two other men to hear me and to come running in my direction. I then slipped away before the men got to me. As I was running away, I looked back and saw them pummeling the other guy that had snuck up behind me. I'm not sure if he is still alive." Leadfoot stared hard at Teddy daring him to interrupt again. Teddy didn't. "And that's all, I swear. I didn't say anything or do anything I wasn't supposed to do."

"The problem is, you saw them kill the first guy. The second guy lived. He was part of their group and was their lookout. He told the other two candle eaters that you saw them kill the first guy. He said you were a road kid. That's why they came here today. They were gonna make sure you never squealed on them. Tumbleweed, they were gonna put you in the bone orchard."

Elizabeth was scared. She hadn't felt that scared in a long time. It didn't seem right for her to be out here on her own like she thought she was capable of doing. She hesitated for a moment and asked, "They were all Russians, right?" The two guys both nodded their heads. "Were any one of them named Nikita? The one that talked to me sounded like a Russian I hoped I'd never see or hear from again?"

Neither Leadfoot nor Teddy would confirm that. The odds were that it wasn't Nikita. There were a lot of Russians out there. But they couldn't be sure. Teddy spoke up after a few moments. "There are a lot of people here, Tumbleweed. You're not gonna last if you let ghosts chase you down the iron rail."

"It's not the ghosts that I'm scared of," she mumbled to herself, even though she looked like she'd seen one.

Leadfoot understood the situation. He felt that quick action needed to be taken. "We may have to leave. We may have to leave soon, like now. Teddy says there's a great chance that they're coming back when everyone is asleep. If they do, well . . . ," his voice trailed off.

Elizabeth leaned up against the tree. "What about everyone else in the hobo jungle? Are they gonna leave, too? They are in danger. Oh my God. I've put them all in danger."

It was Teddy's turn to speak up. "They will stay and protect you whether you are here or not, and the candle eaters know it. They know that that's what we do. We all have each other's back. We're an interesting lot," he said with a crooked smile, "but this is how it works. We are all a single gear that works together to make this machine of a lifestyle work. So don't worry about us. We can handle ourselves. Once the candle eaters realize you're not here they will leave us alone after they leave a few parting bruises. But Leadfoot is right. You have to leave, or the Russians will get you."

Elizabeth left them to talk between themselves. She looked around for some of her things. Thankfully she didn't have much to lose. Her most prized possessions were her weapons, and they never left her sight. She gathered up a few things laying around that no one had claimed, such as a spoon and two cans to cook with for later. She debated about taking the thick blanket that she was using to sleep on. She decided to be selfish and took it. She felt a smidge of guilt, but it had become a luxury item to her. Besides, someone else had taken it from someone else before she had it. She took her things and wrapped them up in her bindle and tied the bindle to her stick.

As she walked out of the hobo jungle, she looked back over her shoulder. Leadfoot and Teddy were in a wildly animated discussion. A few of the hobos acknowledged her with a tip of the hat while others never made eye contact. She wanted to thank the ones that had taken a beating because of her but she knew it wouldn't do any good. This was the hobo way. Everyone had each other's back. It was an unwritten rule that she was learning. One was expected to help out another and in return help was to be given back to you. She had to find a way to help the guys in the jungle. She walked back down to the spot where they had been fishing to think about what she could do. She was sitting there for about fifteen minutes when Leadfoot came clopping through the tall weeds down the embankment.

"Listen," he said, "Teddy's been hearing that those darn candle eaters are planning on showing up just before sunset. They're expecting you and me to leave during the night under the cover of darkness. He also heard that they have a couple guys roaming the train yards and rails. They're on the lookout for a road kid and were told not to let anyone leave by rail."

Elizabeth was silently listening though she never took her eyes off the water. "They're gonna get me aren't they, Leadfoot?"

He was quick to respond, "No, no they won't. Teddy and I have a plan. He went into town to see if there's a chance that he can 'borrow' a horse and one of those work wagons. When he gets one, he's gonna meet me east of town on the other side of the stockyards. You're gonna have to get yourself over that river and across the train tracks without getting caught. Once you get across then you'll have to go down the road until I can meet you. I'll be whistling 'Ole My Darling, Clementine.' When you hear me you whistle it back to me.

Then we'll take off out of this area to maybe, I don't know, somewhere back from where we came from."

Elizabeth still had her eyes on the water. "Can't you take the wagon to the west of town?"

"No. There is no reason for a wagon to be on that side of the town at this time of night. It makes more sense to have it over on the east side by the stockyards where they're stored for the night."

"I don't want to go back the way we came from. If I have to go then I want to go west."

"But you don't know anywhere or anything about that area, Tumbleweed."

"I don't know anything about ANYWHERE, Leadfoot. But I do know that I don't want to go east. That's for sure." She hesitated a moment then said, "You could get hurt. You could get hurt if you're caught with me, Leadfoot. Maybe it's time that we go our own ways." She looked up with watering eyes and could see the hurt in his eyes even though he tried to cover it up with hard facial expressions.

"Don't be silly, Elizabeth." She noticed how he went from calling her Tumbleweed to Elizabeth due to the seriousness of the moment. "They don't have an army throughout the country looking for you. It's just a group of men that are in this place who don't really know who they're looking for. Heck, you could be in the next town, and they would never find you." Elizabeth didn't respond but was still listening. "So, as soon as the sun sets," he continued, "hightail it across the river and tracks and then walk down the road leading out of town. You do know the song, 'My Darling Clementine,' right?"

Her response was a simple nod of the head. She couldn't look back up to face him. So off he went to meet Teddy. Elizabeth sat on the flat rock thinking about what to do. It was odd to her how this day turned out. She started the day by being alone and then relaxing at the river by herself until Leadfoot showed up to fish. She learned how to fish and loved it! She then listened to him and learned how Frank evolved into Leadfoot Frankie. She then forgave him and they became friends once again. Then people got hurt and the jungle got ransacked because of her. Teddy and Leadfoot were now devising a plan to get her out of town.

Now she's back to being alone. This time it might be for a long time. My how the day had come full circle. Elizabeth remembered Teddy teasing her this morning about making sure she wasn't thinking about making a hole in the water . . . That's it! That's what she needed to do. She thought for a few moments. It was going to be dark soon, so she had to hurry. She came up with the plan to fake her drowning. That way no one at the jungle should get hurt by the Russians and she could head off in the direction that she wanted. She pushed some of the rocks and dirt into the river to make it look like she fallen into the water. She also lodged her bindle cloth between two large rocks and then made a new bindle with the thick blanket. It took a few minutes to get the right size, but it seemed to work. Once she was satisfied with the way things looked, she ventured off to the West along the river. Once she was farther away from the hobo jungle, she climbed up the embankment and found a road that seemed alright to follow. Satisfied and yet still uneasy about how the day ended, Elizabeth headed away in a westward direction, whistling "My Darling Clementine."

Being alone wasn't what it was cracked up to be. Elizabeth spent a lot of time doubting every move she made. From the moment that she hit the road she had wished that she'd taken her chance on the train that had slowly gone by a few hours ago. But then she remembered that there could have been one of the Russians on it. Every sound that she heard she swore it was someone tracking her.

She found a giant weeping willow tree and made camp under its long flexible branches that barely swept the ground. It would keep her safe and hidden, but it would also keep her from seeing anyone coming around. She couldn't make a fire. Frankly, she never thought about it. Leadfoot was the one that always started it. She prayed that there would be no rain, but she was pretty confident that the weeping willow tree would provide enough cover. She didn't even unpack her bindle. She kept it packed in case she had to move quickly for some reason. She laid there with exposed blades at the ready just in case.

The sun started to rise in the morning. It reminded her of Leadfoot talking about how the sunrises and sunsets reminded him of his mother. She wished that she had a better way of remembering her mother. But she didn't. There was nothing about her mom that she could think was special. She couldn't even remember a time that her mother or father had made her smile. Leadfoot made her smile. She had smiled and even laughed more in the last month or so than she had for a long, long time.

As the sun pushed itself over the horizon, she pushed herself up and out from under that tree. Her aching muscles and bones screamed to find some soft grass to lay in for a while, but she couldn't. She was hungry and had to find something to eat. It was nice to work and to be able to provide food for herself. It was time to go off and see if she could find a job or some food.

She did not know where she was going. She hoped that she would know it when and if she saw it. So down the road she went. Elizabeth walked all day in the sun with no food or water. She noticed that the road stayed within about a quarter of a mile of the railroad track for a long while, but they were separating at a greater distance the further she traveled. She felt that if she stayed on the road it would lead to a town and maybe some farms. The rail would be a lot quicker than walking, but the train does not always stop at all towns.

Eventually, as she kept walking the rail became further and further away from the road. Who knew when the next train would come by? So, she stayed on the road. Later on that day she saw a farmhouse in the distance. She walked up the dirt lane that led to the house and two barns. Once she got closer to one of the barns she noticed a marking on a fence post. "I wonder what that symbol means," she said it louder than she thought.

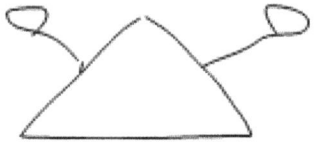

A farmer heard her speak as he was walking out of the barn. He went over to see what she was doing. He was a big guy with overalls covering only bare skin. The stitching looked like it could give away at any moment from the girth under the fabric. "What do you want?" the farmer barked. His mustache covered his mouth. You couldn't see his mouth at all.

Elizabeth put on a huge smile and waved way too eagerly, "Hello, my name is Elizabeth. I was hoping that you had some chores for me to do. I thought maybe you could pay me with a little food and water, if that's agreeable to you."

The farmer grunted with the compassion of a lead pipe. "Ain't no chore for you to do and there sure ain't no food. You can stick your face in the horse trough if you need waterin'. Then I'll kindly ask for you to leave the way you came."

Dejected as she was, Elizabeth went over to the trough and bent over to drink the water. There was a film on top of it with pieces of hay and dead flies floating in it. How many horses had stuck their nose in there? She stuck her cupped hands deep into the trough hoping that the water was cleaner in the middle. After a couple handfuls she thought she'd put on a little charm. It didn't work. "I saw that marking on the fence post. Did a hobo put that there? It must be a real privilege for them to have someone like you to help them, uh, us. I know for a fact I'm appreciative of your kind, generous nature. What's it code for anyway?"

The farmer was losing his patience with her, "You haven't been on the trail all that long, have you? You're a tenderfoot, is that what they call you? Well, I'll tell ya one thing, your innocence is what's keeping you from having holes blown right through you. I've learned over time that that symbol means 'man with a gun' for your type of people and I carved it in there to keep you people away from my property. Now it's time for you to leave."

Elizabeth knew it was time. She was embarrassed and scared but couldn't hold her tongue. As she walked away, she turned towards him and opened her mouth, "Man with a gun? No way you have a gun. You're too fat to have a gun under those coveralls. I don't know. I guess you could hide a gun under that belly fat that's sticking out the edges of your overalls." As she was squawking at him, she didn't notice that he reached inside the barn door and withdrew a shotgun. "As a matter of fact," she continued, "you're so fat there's no way you could run fast to get a gun before I stole some eggs out of your hen-hou . . . " CCCRRAACCCKKK. The air above her head was shattered with buckshot. The farmer had quickly reloaded another shell, but he didn't need to aim towards her and pull the trigger because she was already two thirds down the lane leading to the main road. He giggled to himself, although he was also concerned for the way she was living. He believed that living on the road and seeking handouts was no life for a young person.

Elizabeth was pissed. She had mad tears burning trails down her face. She was hungry and tired and hot. She walked a few miles down the road occasionally checking over her shoulder to make sure that the crazy farmer wasn't following her. Eventually she reached a meadow of really soft grass. She owed her bones and muscles a little relaxation, so she went over to it and sprawled down in it.

Just for a moment.

Just for a few minutes.

Just for a little while.

Elizabeth opened her eyes and saw nothing but complete darkness. And twinkling stars. Thousands and thousands of them. She wondered if maybe one of them was her own mother looking down on her just as Leadfoot's mother was in the sunrises and sunsets and the small ripples in the water. The wonderment of those thoughts led her to a deep and welcoming sleep.

* * *

The rest of the week was uneventful for Tumbleweed, that is if you call unsuccessfully jumping on a slow-moving train, not once, but twice, uneventful. There were also hours and hours of walking on tired feet followed by pulling weeds out of a garden all afternoon for an elderly woman. Her only reward for the loathsome job was one ham sandwich with a molding tomato that she devoured in seconds. She had even stopped at a hobo jungle later that evening with some terrifying looking people wandering about. She had quickly decided to leave and took her chances on her own under the stars again. Leadfoot had always said that there is strength in numbers. But by the way this group of men had been ogling her, she felt unquestionably safer on her own that night. So, if you could call all of this humdrum and routine, then yes, not much had happened.

She woke up before dawn and debated whether to try her luck jumping the next train or to just stay on the road. Both had their advantages and disadvantages. The flattened dirt road was easier on her feet than the rocky and unleveled railroad track ground. Her shoes were becoming well worn. She decided that the road would cause less wear and tear on them. Besides, the track had begun to frequently run through lonelier deserted areas. So, she continued her walk west. After hours of walking along the road, the late summer sun still beat down on her.

Doubt began to creep into her psyche when she heard a distant train whistle. The train was heading east. It seemed that it was going back to where she had left some days ago. Her doubt had turned into contemplation about whether to go back. Hopefully she could find Leadfoot or even Toledo Teddy. Maybe they were still in the city working. Hopefully she could get her old job back. Maybe they were gone. Maybe all the Russian transients were still there and waiting for her to come back. She could hear Leadfoot saying that anybody can go back from where they came from. That's the easiest thing to do. He would say that it's more adventurous to go towards the unknown. And, well, she's on an adventure, so she kept walking west, though she thought a little familiarity would be nice about now. She missed Leadfoot. She missed him a lot. Perhaps being alone wasn't all that it was cracked up to be. But hey, if you never go, you will never know.

She came upon a farm. She was able to convince the farmer's wife to let her spend most of the afternoon helping her gather eggs from a chicken coop and a few other dull chores that could be performed in hope of getting some food to eat. As she brought a basket of eggs into the kitchen, she saw the wife was baking a pie for her husband who was tending to some cornfields.

The farmer's wife had offered her a bath for her labor. The wife was sure that her husband would be okay with her sleeping in the hayloft for the night. Elizabeth decided to quickly get herself cleaned up before the farmer came home. When she was finished, the wife gave her a supper consisting of pork and beans with cornbread. Elizabeth had learned through the weeks to keep some food for later, so she stashed away the cornbread.

She also thought it would be best that she wouldn't be around when the farmer came home so she went into the dusty hayloft to get out of the sun. As she laid on the soft hay, she scanned the inside of the barn. It was mainly used to store bales of hay. She didn't see any useful tools. She noticed a machine with a spool of thick string attached to it. She presumed that it was used to tie bales of hay. She jumped down from the loft and took a bunch of string from the machine and stashed it in her bindle. She wasn't sure if she'd ever need it but thought it could be useful.

Elizabeth heard the farmer come back from the fields with his team of horses and wagon. He hitched them up to a post at the water trough. A few minutes later she could hear the farmer and his wife loudly arguing. She knew the argument was about her so she got down from the hayloft and walked around towards the near side of the house totally out of sight. As she stood by the house, she saw the farmer walk towards the outhouse just as the wife walked toward the barn. She knew that the wife was going there to tell her that she had to leave. She couldn't bear to hear that she was being forced to leave once again.

She didn't hang around to hear it.

She just left.

She left with a cherry pie.

Elizabeth kept walking west to an unknown destination. She had learned earlier that it wasn't safe for a young girl to be walking along the road by herself so whenever she caught a glimpse of someone coming towards her, she would duck into the nearest woods or cornfield and wait for them to pass. She would then jump back on the road.

That evening after a traveler had passed her, she jumped over a fallen branch to get back onto the road. She didn't succeed in her leap and tripped and fell into the branch. She skinned herself up pretty badly, but she would be okay. The damage that was caused was to her right shoe. The branch had caught the sole of the shoe and left the heel barely hanging on. When she dusted herself off and started walking down the dirt road, she noticed that the heel limply hung on to the shoe just waiting to fall off. She had to slightly drag her right foot so the shoe wouldn't fall apart. Frustration overcame her for she knew she couldn't walk any distance with only one good shoe. She had no idea exactly where she was or where she could get a new shoe. Darkness had now overtaken the day, so she decided to sit in her own pity and soon fell asleep just off the road under a tree.

Dawn set in and there was a scent of rain in the air. Elizabeth wasn't sure what to do. She didn't want to get caught out in the rain, but she had to stay on the move. She wished that she had jumped the train earlier yesterday. At least her shoe wouldn't have fallen apart. It didn't matter. She had made the decision to stay on the road and now she had to live with it at least until she came to the next railroad crossing. She stayed under the tree and ate half of the cornbread that she stashed away from last night's meal. She thought about that delicious cherry pie that she pilfered from the farmer. She felt bad about taking it. But man, was it delicious!

Rain clouds had kept their distance. She decided to chance it and started walking down the road. Her broken shoe was giving her fits until she remembered the string that she had taken from the baler machine in the barn. Now she was excited. She pulled some of it out and chewed off a good length of it from the fistful that she'd taken. It took a while gnawing at it, but it finally broke loose. She began wrapping it around the heel and sole of her shoe. It looked like it would only hold temporarily, but it was better than nothing. She had a little more pep in her step from her string idea. It was a little personal battle that she won, but it was a huge confidence booster.

She continued ambling down the dirt road. It hadn't rained yet, but the promising dark clouds let her know that at any given point it would unload on her. She was tired and decided that she would stop in the next town she came to and wait until a train pulled in. She didn't know how but she was determined to jump on that steam hog. She took a break on a big rock and fished out the remaining cornbread from yesterday. She noticed a small town up ahead of her. She guessed it was about an hour's walk away. She rested for a moment and then worked her way to the town. Maybe she could find quick work for some supper.

She had just sat down on the rock and began nibbling on the last morsel of her cornbread when she heard the whinnying and braying of a mule. She looked back at the direction that she came from and noticed a mule pulling a wagon with one man on it. She quickly slid off the rock and took the end off her bindle stick exposing the blade. She thought for a moment that she could rob the man of his mule and wagon, but then thought against doing that. She didn't know how to drive a wagon let alone deal with a potential stubborn mule. So, she just hid and waited for them to pass just like all the other times.

But wait! What was that sound?

The man was whistling.

He was whistling, "Oh My Darling, Clementine!"

Elizabeth remembered that Leadfoot had planned on meeting up with her the night she left. Only she didn't go the direction as planned. What were the odds that this was Leadfoot on the wagon? "Oh My Darling, Clementine" was the latest catchy tune of the time. Surely everyone knew that song. She had to take the chance. The wagon came up to her and the driver was still whistling that tune. She stayed hidden but whistled it back to him just as he passed, that way she had the advantage of being behind him and could escape if the driver ended up being a bad apple. As soon as she whistled one short line of the tune the driver yelled, "Whoa, whoa!" The mule hee-hawed in defiance, and slowly came to a halt. The man grabbed a long blade off his lap and turned and pointed at the figure behind the rock. "Tumbleweed?"

Elizabeth jumped out from behind the rock leading with the point of her blade. "Leadfoot?" It was all she asked even though she knew the answer. Leadfoot slid off the side of the wagon. He caught her with a swoop of his arms. They stood there in a strong bear hug that seemed to last forever. She hadn't seen him for days, but it felt more like months. He felt like he'd found a long-lost friend.

Eventually, he let go of her and gave her a once-over look to see if she was alright. She was okay to his satisfaction. He then excitedly spoke, "What happened to you that night?" Before she could answer, he continued, "I waited as long as I could. After a while, I couldn't wait any longer. I had to leave because all hell was about to break loose. I was hoping that you snuck away but then I got worried that you couldn't find me, so I went on down the road whistling like a steam kettle. I whistled that tune for miles. Teddy had 'borrowed' this wagon and mule from the stockyard for our escape. I would have gladly taken a horse, but Teddy felt like he was closely watched. After a day or so of riding east with this obstinate animal pulling this wagon only when it wanted, I feared that you decided to hitch a ride on a steam hog. If that was the case, then I knew it was practically impossible to meet up with you. I was told that a couple of the candle eaters were seen searching the rail yards and had even jumped on and off the trains searching for a road kid."

Leadfoot kept talking as he pulled a bunch of carrots from the back of the wagon and fed them to the mule. "Then Teddy found me and told me that a small group of Russians had come to the hobo jungle looking to cause some trouble just as they had planned. They were taken down to the river and shown where it looked like you fell in and you were never found. It was hard for me not to chuckle when I heard that. I knew you staged it so you could get away. Then I remembered us talking about a town called Harrisburg in Indiana.

I took a shot that that may be where you were heading. So, I turned this here mule around and took a western course to try to locate you." He threw the carrot greens and stems into the grass and produced a turnip for the mule to eat.

"So how did you find me? How did you know that I wasn't on a train heading west?"

"I didn't. Frankly, it was just dumb luck. I traveled west until I came upon a farm. I asked a grumpy nasty farmer if he would provide some water for this here mule. I said that I'd even work for it if he insisted on it. He told me to scram. He said that he had just ran one worthless soul off his property. I hoped that soul was you. I guess I wasn't moving fast enough for his liking, so he shot over my head. That scared this stubborn beast. He was so fearful that he pulled away from my grasp and raced haphazardly towards the farmer's garden. The farmer aimed his shotgun at the mule. I knocked that clover kicker out cold with a fist to the jaw right before he could fire at the mule. I had to lure the beast out of the garden with some carrots. On our way out, we stopped at the water pump and used a water bucket for the mule to take a long drink. Then we proceeded westward whistling that tune and hoping for a response. Then lo and behold, I heard a response for the first time in days and there you were!"

They both got on the wagon to search for some water for the mule. They found a stream that was easy to get to. Leadfoot untied the animal, and they led him down to the stream. The impending storm didn't seem to be coming their direction. She followed him as he led the mule back to the wagon and buckled it into the harness. "Well . . . " hesitated Leadfoot, "that storm seems to be behind us and going away from us." He uncomfortably shifted from one foot to another. "I suppose it may be time for me to head out . . ."

"Oh, quit dallying about, Leadfoot," an impatient Elizabeth said. "Since you can't come out and ask me, then I guess I'll say it. I would like to ride with you if that's alright." She tried to act as normal as possible, but inside she was scared that he would say no.

Leadfoot chuckled and said, "I kinda thought you would, but I wasn't sure of your plans." He hopped up on the seat and motioned Elizabeth up next to him. She gladly jumped up onto the seat with ease.

"Wow, that was easier than hopping onto a train," she joked.

Leadfoot laughed and said, "I was gonna ask you if you wanted to get off and allow me to get a head start moving this wagon so you could run and time your jump on it."

"I doubt that I could jump anywhere with the way this shoe is coming apart." Leadfoot leaned over to look at it.

"There's a town up ahead. I bet I can find you a better pair of shoes."

"Then let's head that way. Maybe we can find some food."

Elizabeth had earlier guessed that the small town was about an hour's walk away. That was before she knew she was going to be treated like a queen and be carried in a mule driven wagon. They got there in half the time. "Don't get too used to the speed of this mule. He is so doggone stubborn. Heck the other day I only got about five hours out of him until he flat sat down in the middle of the road. He wouldn't eat or drink anything. Just plain ole obstinate."

Leadfoot pulled up in front of a church. He hitched the mule and wagon onto a post and then escorted Elizabeth inside the church. Once inside they found the minister and told him their story. Leadfoot felt that most churches and ministers want to help the poor by providing necessities to the neediest in society. This minister went above and beyond their expectations. He provided food and water for them and also for the mule. He provided an extra shirt and socks and especially shoes for Elizabeth. They each received a small blanket. The minister told them the Word of God during their lunch, and that was okay. They found it quite interesting, especially Elizabeth. She had never attended church. They both felt better and more at peace from the message.

Leadfoot and Elizabeth insisted on earning their keep by doing a couple chores around the church. They didn't want the minister to think that they were bums or tramps. Realizing how determined they were to give back, the minister found a couple jobs for each of them to do. He even provided them a place to sleep inside the church for the night. As they were planning on leaving the next morning, the minister gave Elizabeth a small cross carved out of wood. She was grateful for her gift and planned on making it into a necklace as soon as she could. The minister would tell a parishioner later the next day that he was most pleased with these two people. It was nice to see people being thankful for what they have and helping others.

As the two left the small town by the mule pulling the wagon, Elizabeth made a mental note of this place and especially the church. She also carved her first hobo symbol on the hitching post:

Craig Leavitt

13

They traveled most of the morning in silence. The silence wasn't a strained silence, but more of a calm relaxation. Even the mule seemed tranquil and appeased as Leadfoot reigned him along the dirt road. Elizabeth sat beside him as she blankly stared at the passing scenery. Her mind was somewhere else while she fingered the wooden cross that the minister had given her. Leadfoot looked over at her a few times as he led the mule down the road.

"What are you frettin' over, young lady?" He asked.

Elizabeth didn't directly answer him. She just kept stroking the wooden cross. A few moments later she said, "I never told you why I left without telling you. I suppose, in the least, I owe that to you." He waited for a moment before he responded.

"I figured you'd tell me when you wanted to. A part of me feared to know the reason. I thought maybe you grew tired of having me around. But then again, people come and go in this way of life. It's hard to get used to at times." Elizabeth listened to him and kept her head down. She didn't want him to see her eyes welling up with tears. "After a couple of days, I figured you'd made your decision about finding me and the wagon. That's when I headed west in search of you. I felt that you're not ready to be out here alone just yet and I hoped that I'd find you. Like I said earlier, if you had jumped a train, I doubt that I'd be able to. I didn't have anything to lose, so I headed out on the main stem heading west, hoping to find you."

"I left to protect you," she said.

"Protect me? Protect me from what?"

"I felt that I had created the situation by sneaking and watching those men kill that guy. People had gotten hurt at the hobo jungle because of me and if I stayed there, then even more would have gotten hurt." She took a long breath and then continued. "I couldn't bear the thought of you getting hurt. You've been so good to me. It would've killed me if I knew that you had gotten hurt because of something I'd done. So, I left. I had been thinking a lot about going it alone recently. I figured many others have been out there alone, so why not me. After seeing what the other men had done to protect me, I figured that I'd never really be alone. Someone would always have my back." Leadfoot didn't respond. He knew she had to get her feelings talked out. She was wiser than she should be considering her age. He knew it . . . and he knew she was about to know it too.

"If there was ever going to be a perfect time for me to leave on my own, then that was the time. I just assumed that the Russians knew that we were friends and had seen us together and if they didn't know, then they would soon figure it out. I thought that if I left without meeting you, then maybe the guys that were looking for me wouldn't harass you. My reaction for everything that was going on was to take action and leave. It was time to learn about myself. I've never been alone, and no time was better than then. I thought that I could sustain myself with some of the skills that I'd learned from you.

I knew that there would be hardships with my newfound freedom, but hey, my life hasn't ever been a cakewalk. How much worse could it get? Well, after a while I began to realize that I just might not be built to be alone." Elizabeth then went on and told him about her experiences in the last week or so. He just listened in silence. Then she launched into telling her newest stories to him. When she finished, Leadfoot led the mule towards some large shady oak trees for a quick rest. He looked over at her and could tell that she was fretting over something.

"What is it, Elizabeth? What's on your mind?"

Her reply was conflicted. "I don't know. I feel like I need something but I'm not sure what it is. I feel that something is missing. Being out here on the road is nice. It's nice to know that I can come and go wherever and whenever I want to. But there's something missing."

Leadfoot looked at her for a long moment. "Stability?"

"Huh? What do you mean?" Elizabeth was not quite paying attention. She had been in deep thought.

"Stability. I think that's what you think you need. Consistency, safety, balance. This way life is a difficult one. It takes a long time to find your way in it. Some souls are just not cut out for it."

"How did you realize that you were made for this way of life?"

Leadfoot let out a slight sigh. "I just did. I could take care of myself. Sure, I had my bad days out on the rail. But that just told me that there was a good one just around the bend. I'm also a big guy.

Not very many people are gonna mess with me. You, on the other hand, are not much of a threat."

Elizabeth was taken back by Leadfoot's comment. She jumped off the wagon and stood in the grass. "For God's sake, Leadfoot, I killed a man! You call that not being a threat?" Leadfoot looked over his shoulders towards a line of trees and hoped no one was there to hear what she just said. He then attempted to calm her down. He tried to explain to her that it isn't smart to announce that in public. You never know who's within earshot.

"I'm not saying," he explained, "that you can't take care of yourself. I'm saying that you don't scare or awe people. Remember when we showed up in that hobo camp? No one feared you."

"But the other men respected me."

"That's right. They were being civil and courteous to a fellow hobo. No one was in awe, Elizabeth. I'm sure most of them could tell you were a fresh road kid." She quietly mulled over that for a while. Leadfoot continued, "What I was trying to say earlier is that you may be suited for a more day to day routine. Maybe something similar to what you had back in Boston, but not exactly," he added. He saw the look on her face turn fearful when he made that last comment. Surely, she had suddenly thought of the big Russian, Nikita. After sitting there for a few more moments, he got up and got the mule and the wagon turned back towards the dirt road. It took a little coaxing, but the beast began to lead the way. "So, what are your thoughts? Do we stay on the road with the mule and wagon, or do we pull into the next town and sell the stubborn beast and jump on the next steam hog out of town?"

The thought of jumping another train didn't sound appetizing to Elizabeth at all. Then she recollected something that she heard. "Back when we were in the hobo jungle," she began, "I remember a couple of ornery hobos comparing that town to another town in Indiana. It was something like Harrisburg or Harrison."

"Yeah, I remember that. It was Harrisburg. Remember earlier I told you that's where I thought you were heading? Anyway, yeah, I worked with them on occasion in town loading wagons with supplies," he said. "There was a train coming in the rail yard from Fort Wayne. They had gotten to town by hopping off a Pennsy steamer leaving Harrisburg via Fort Wayne. They talked about how they wished that they had stayed in that small up-and-coming town. They said there was a lot of work there and fewer nasty immigrants at that time. I reckon that they would take a catch back if they could stay sober long enough."

"Catch back?"

"Yeah, it means to ride a train back from where a person came. I thought that was pretty obvious," he teased.

"Anyway," Elizabeth went on trying to ignore his wisecrack, "so I was thinking maybe we could head that way and check it out? It would give us a goal besides meandering through the countryside looking for our next meal."

Leadfoot thought about that for a moment without saying anything as he led the mule down the road. Elizabeth added, "I just think I need an objective to get me out of this funk I'm beginning to sink into. So, what do you say? We already have a wagon and a mule. There would be no reason to hop a freight."

"Yeah, but we could get there a whole lot faster by rail," he countered. It was obvious Leadfoot loved his train riding.

"Faster if we knew where the train was exactly heading. It could take days to find the right one and successfully stick a landing on it." Elizabeth was getting excited with the talk of a plan.

Leadfoot gave in to her idea. "Then Harrisburg, Indiana is the destination!" He shouted. And for good measure he threw in a "Hey-ah." The mule just grunted and proceeded with his normal gait.

The road to Harrisburg wasn't quite a direct road. The trip had many twists and turns. There were giant tree-topped hills. They had to coax the mule to zigzag along the narrow trail. At one time they thought that they would have to leave the wagon because they didn't think that it would fit between some of the trees that stood guard of the twisty path.

They eventually made it through the forests, and the road turned into a gravelly terrain. So gravelly that the wagon would sink into it and act like it was stuck in mud. The mule had a hard time pulling it out. A couple of times they had to hop off and help the mule pull the wagon out. These were the times that an irritable Leadfoot would remind Elizabeth that they could be flying down a rail in a boxcar. There were times that the road would slowly change into a small path that would eventually turn into a nonexistent trail. For most of one day they stayed as close to a river as they could because the ground was easier to travel. A few days later, they meandered through a meadow because the road or path simply was nowhere to be found.

These were the days that tried Leadfoot's patience. At those times he was never sure if they were on private property or not. He hoped that they wouldn't find out that they were by having to pick buckshot out of their hide from a shotgun of an angry clover kicker. Luckily that was never the case. Eventually the terrain became somewhat normal and their pace quickened. Quickened as much as a crotchety mule would allow.

Leadfoot begged and pleaded, "Come on you mangy beast! Let's go! You've pulled this cart all day! We just have a couple hundred feet yet to go then you can rest for the evening!" The creature wouldn't budge. They had finally reached the bridge that crossed the river between Jonesboro and Harrisburg.

"C'mon, get moving!" A man yelled from behind them. The angry man had a wagon full of wooden boxes and barrels stacked precariously high and was needing to get across the river to Harrisburg. "The day is coming to an end and I ain't got time to wait on y'all!"

Leadfoot was exasperated with the current situation. Mules are known for their stubbornness, but for the last week or so, the animal hadn't really given them much trouble. Throughout the journey it had mostly been agreeable until now. The mule refused to budge . . . literally. "I don't know what the problem is with this mule," He moaned as Elizabeth jumped out of the wagon and tried to no avail, pulling the mule along by its reins onto the bridge. He put both feet on the bridge and backed off as quickly as he had put them on it.

Another man rode up on his horse to see what was the hold-up. He tied his horse to a post at the entrance of the bridge and walked up to Leadfoot, Elizabeth and the stubborn beast. "I had the same problem with my young mare a while back," the man offered. "I think the problem may be that the mule doesn't like the movement of that rickety bridge while pulling the wagon." The bridge was narrow, but just wide enough for two wagons to cross at the same time. Though it was sturdy, it was made of heavy rope and wooden boards for the floor. This type of structure caused a slight sway to the bridge. To an apprehensive animal, it was more of a swing and wobble that was not like solid ground. "If you don't mind my help, I'll pull your wagon across the bridge with my mare." Elizabeth wasn't sure if she trusted him.

"What's in it for you, Mister?" she asked.

The man laughed, "There's nothing in it for me at all. But it'll sure stop you guys from being cussed at by these other folks trying to get across the bridge."

Elizabeth walked over towards Leadfoot who was at the head of the mule. "I don't know. I think if we prodded the mule a little more, I'm sure we could . . . " Leadfoot had had enough. As Elizabeth was talking he disconnected the beast from the wagon. The helpful man walked back to his horse and then hooked her up to their wagon. Elizabeth just chuckled. She couldn't be mad at Leadfoot. She understood his frustration.

It had been a long journey. Eventually they got across the bridge and the traffic started moving. Leadfoot and the man switched out animals and got everything put back in order. Elizabeth noticed that there were some people and campfires down along the Harrisburg side of the river. The smell from the smoke wafting through the air triggered their stomachs to growl. They decided to make camp near the others.

They invited the friendly man to stay and have something to eat. He was obliged and even offered to add a little of what he had for the animals. As they ate, they told him why they came to Harrisburg and a little of what their lives were like in the recent days. They learned that the man's name was Robert Wymer, and he owned a farm where he milked cows. He also delivered the milk to Jonesboro and surrounding areas. "Harrisburg is booming with the discovery of natural gas. I love being able provide the milk to this town. Especially with the expected population explosion that's happening. I can't imagine the extra work it would take to deliver all that milk. I'd have to build up my equipment, but I know it would be a profitable venture."

Elizabeth added, "I sure wouldn't want to pull a loaded wagon across that bridge all day long. That thing rocks too much for me."

Robert softly laughed at her comment. "Yeah, that's a valid point, but that's a risk I'd be willing to take. I don't know if you noticed, but if you look back over to the near side of the bridge, you'll see a lot of stacked wood there. They should be starting to build a much sturdier, stronger wooden covered bridge. You see, as I said earlier, natural gas fields have been found on this side of the river. Enough gas to provide power to thousands of people, some say tens of thousands of people."

Elizabeth was getting a little excited. "Yes," she quickly spoke, "when we were in Ohio, we heard that a small town in Indiana was becoming somewhat of a boomtown." Leadfoot listened intently as he stoked the fire.

"Well, you're partially right, young lady," Robert said. "Harrisburg IS a boomtown! I'm hearing of factories that produce all types of things planning to move here with the promise of free gas if they come. I'm telling you, this place is gonna be big! I even bought my cousin Jack's land way out east of Harrisburg. I plan on making a dairy farm on it as soon as I'm clear more of the land." That comment made Elizabeth and Leadfoot exchange a glance. After a few more minutes talking to each other Robert got up to leave. He climbed up on and pointed his horse towards the river and proceeded to cross it.

"Hey," yelled Elizabeth, "shouldn't you go up and cross at the bridge?"

"Nah," shouted back Robert, "the river is only a couple feet deep right here this time of the year. Normally I wouldn't attempt it at all, but I'm sure the cool water will be refreshing to her. Besides," Robert added, "there's a small line of wagons waiting to cross the bridge and I don't wanna wait." He sighed, "Boy, I sure can't wait for that wooden covered bridge to be built." Once he forded the river, he yelled back at the two, "If you two have time in the next couple of days, come on out to my farm. It's easy to find. Cross over this river and follow the trail due south. You can't miss it. If the wind is blowing the right direction, you'll probably smell it before you see it." Leadfoot grinned. He knew what that meant.

"What are you grinning at, Leadfoot? I don't understand. Milk doesn't smell."

Leadfoot responded to her with a chuckle, "That's right, Tumbleweed, it doesn't. But the milk producers do."

T he sun had been up for a few hours as they began their way to the farm. They soon noticed that Robert wasn't wrong with what he said when he left them the night before. They could smell the dairy farm as soon as they left the town limits of Jonesboro and Harrisburg. The trip was a short one, even with a stubborn mule. The dairy farm was big and had a lot of area to expand. As they rode upon the property, Robert was walking out of one of the barns. He had been unloading milk jugs from the back of a wagon. A horse was in the background eating from a pile of hay. Elizabeth waved as they pulled up to Robert's wagon.

"Dad-gum you showed up," said Robert. "I wasn't sure if you two would take me up on my offer." Elizabeth jumped down from the wagon and went over to pet Robert's horse as it ate. She then grabbed a handful of hay and fed the mule after she got the okay from Robert. After they talked for a few minutes, Robert showed them around the farm. Elizabeth was amazed by the size of the two barns that allowed the cows shelter from the heat, but otherwise they roamed the near pasture. Another barn had farm equipment. There was another outbuilding that housed milk jugs and bottles and such. This was where they were cleaned, stacked, and stored.

After the tour, Robert took them to the front of the wraparound porch of the house. There were two tall shade trees that hung over the porch. His wife had gone to visit her sister in Muncie. She was to return in the next few days. Luckily, she had made meals for him to eat during her absence. So, they sat in the shade on the porch eating sandwiches and drinking sweet tea. Robert asked them how long they had planned on staying in the area.

"Well, that all really depends," Elizabeth hesitated as she looked at Leadfoot for reassurance. "It all depends on how things work here out in Harrisburg. I'm not too sure if I'm built to be living on the road. It's an adventure, yes, but I think I want to slow down a bit. You know, stick my feet in the dirt and see if they take root." After a little more talking about the area and what kind of jobs that were available, Robert offered to let them stay a day or two and loaf around if they wanted. They decided to accept the offer.

"Except there won't be any loafing from us," Leadfoot said. "We want to earn our keep." So, it was decided that they would stay until Robert's wife returned from her visit with her sister and in the meantime, would give a hand or two . . . or four, with things that needed to be done. There was raking and piling of the hay for the cows, washing milk jugs and bottles and then stacking them in crates. Robert asked Leadfoot if he'd be willing to stack firewood that was piled up at the edge of the woods. So he used the stubborn mule and wagon and ventured off to the woods to get the wood.

In the meantime, Elizabeth had been inquisitive about how to milk cows. Robert gave her a quick demonstration but told her the real test would be very early in the morning. She was welcome to help him at that time and she happily accepted. Robert and Elizabeth helped Leadfoot when he returned with the wood.

Leadfoot held a couple of water buckets as Elizabeth pumped long strokes to draw the water up from the well. They took turns in the barn, cleaned themselves up and then ate some dinner with Robert. He offered them each a bedroom for the night, but Leadfoot quickly declined. He said that they would be just as comfortable in the barn. Elizabeth was disappointed but agreed to stay in the barn with him. As nightfall flooded in on the farm, Robert went to bed and they went to the barn. Elizabeth piled some blankets in the back of the wagon as she prepared for bed. Leadfoot made a thick pile of hay for his bed that night. Elizabeth gazed out the barn door at stars and then asked him, "Hey, why did you so quickly decline the offer to sleep on a real bed under a real roof? It would have been much more comfortable." She thought she better ask him before the snoring began.

He was quiet for a few moments before he answered. "Well, Tumbleweed, we haven't been under a roof of any type since we were on those cots in that church in Ohio. In fact, I couldn't even tell you a time before that that we were lucky enough to have one. It had always been sleeping under the stars, in a barn, in a tent or under the trees." She listened to him as he continued after a long pause. "I don't want to get used to that comfort feeling, Elizabeth. As much as I love the amenity of a simple thing such as a bed or a roof, I don't yearn for that as much as I loathe the despair of losing it. If I don't have it, then I don't long for it."

"I would think that being on the road and rail for as long as you have, you would want to find someplace to settle down. Don't you get tired of always being on the move?"

Leadfoot thought for a few moments before he answered. "Being on the move is what I do. I've done it for so long. It became what I do. It's become what I am."

* * *

They woke early the next morning with Robert banging the side of a cast iron bell that hung from a wooden post in the ground. Elizabeth jumped straight out of the wagon and nearly out of her skin from all the clamoring. Leadfoot lazily rolled over and got up and leaned against the side of the barn door.

"Sorry to startle you two," laughed Robert. "I always ring the bell in the morning after I wake up. I believe it's a signal to the cows to prepare themselves for milkin'. Leadfoot, sir, if you wouldn't mind, could you bring the horse and wagon over to the barn so we can load up the milk. I'm gonna show Elizabeth here what it takes to milk a cow. Afterwards, we'll get some breakfast and then I'll head out on the route."

They obliged Robert in what he asked and got to work. He showed Elizabeth how to milk a cow. She was clumsy at first, but she was a fast learner. She and Robert quickly finished the job. Leadfoot had the milk distributed to where it needed to be, and the wagon was stocked and loaded in record time. After a quick breakfast of eggs and bacon, Robert was preparing to head off on the route. "You two are welcomed to come along if you want," he said. Neither had anything else to do. They jumped up in the wagon with Elizabeth in the back and Leadfoot riding shotgun.

They had been doing the milk route for about an hour. They met a lot of new people in town. Most of them were friendly, but of course, there were a few that turned up their noses at them, especially when they saw the bedraggled Leadfoot. He just smiled. He was used to that look. The three had stopped at the far edge of town to get a refill of water in their canteens. "Say, while we're over on this side of town," Robert said, "let me take you two over to the land I bought from my cousin and show you the layout." Elizabeth said a quick yes before Leadfoot could shoot it down.

"If it doesn't offend you, Robert," Leadfoot said, "I think I'll stroll around town for a while. At one of our earlier stops, I overheard a couple of men talking about some bricking laying jobs."

"No, not at all. I like a man with ambition. Do you have a background in bricklaying?" Asked Robert.

"Yeah," he answered, "You could say I have some experience in it." Elizabeth giggled. She knew his knowledge in bricklaying. So Leadfoot went back into town on foot to look into a possible job. Robert continued to his land with Elizabeth. He presumed that she wouldn't be that interested, but he was pleasantly surprised by how into it she was. He pointed out ideas that they had on the layout of the new farm, and she had a few questions. He was excited to answer them.

Robert and Elizabeth finished the milk route and went back to the Wymer farm. There was no sign of Leadfoot, so they decided to start the next round of daily chores. Elizabeth showed great interest in all the workings of the farm. Robert noticed it and made mental notes about her so he could relate them later to his wife. The rest of the evening went just like the night before. The next morning started out again with the ringing of that cast iron bell. But today they had to work extra quick since they had to pick up Robert's wife from the train station. That was okay for Leadfoot. He wanted to go back into town after noon to check on some things.

Everything was successfully done before afternoon. Elizabeth accompanied Robert to the train station in Harrisburg to wait for his wife to show. The train from Muncie arrived right on time with the love of Robert's life. He gave her a great big hug as she strained to lean up to give him a kiss on the cheek. Elizabeth smiled as Robert gathered his wife's belongings as she grabbed his arm. He whispered something into his wife's ear as they proceeded towards Elizabeth and then stopped in front of her. She smiled at Elizabeth. "My, my, my. And who do we have here?"

Robert opened his mouth to answer, but Elizabeth beat him to the punch. "Hello," she said as she stuck out her hand, "my name is Elizabeth. Elizabeth Byrne." Wow, she thought to herself. That's the first time in a long time she had used her last name. Is it still actually her last name, she wondered?

"Hello, Elizabeth Byrne, my name is Ellen Wymer. It's a pleasure to meet you," she said before Robert could speak. Ellen told Robert all about her trip and time in Muncie as they walked to the horse and wagon. Robert explained to Ellen about coming upon Elizabeth and Leadfoot as they trekked back to their farm. When they got there, Leadfoot walked out from behind the storage barn and gave Ellen quite a start. Coming home and seeing a stranger walking on her property was not something she was used to. They introduced Leadfoot to Ellen. After everyone was acquainted, Leadfoot and Elizabeth finished up some chores so that Robert and Ellen could spend some time together back in the house. Leadfoot had earlier told Robert that he and Elizabeth could go and find their own food and place to stay for the night. Robert wouldn't hear of any such nonsense and that they were welcomed to stay in the house to eat and sleep. Leadfoot got Robert to agree for them to eat and sleep in the barn one more night. He believed that it would make Ellen feel awkward to have strangers sleeping under her roof and it was agreed . . . for now.

Leadfoot and Elizabeth were sleeping in their usual places in the barn. Elizabeth was fingering the small cross that she received from the minister in Ohio when she heard Leadfoot say, "I got some good news and some bad news, Tumbleweed."

She leaned up on one elbow. "Really? What's the good news? I want that first."

He hesitated for a moment and then said, "I got a job today."

"Good news? That's great news! You got a job! That was quick! How did that happen?"

"Well, it was rather sudden. When the three of us traveled through Harrisburg, I noticed a couple of guys that we worked with in Ohio. I went to talk to them, and they sent me to this job pusher. They stood behind my work, and I got offered a job. I start tomorrow."

Elizabeth was so excited for Leadfoot, but she was a little apprehensive because he wouldn't look at her. He just kept staring at the hayloft. Him having a job and Elizabeth not having one yet was a mite troublesome, but nothing serious that couldn't be fixed. "So, what's the bad news?"

He breathed out a cleansing breath and then said, "The job requires very long hours. Robert was right when he told us the other day that they are expecting Harrisburg's population to boom. And I mean boom. There is gonna be a big need for bricks for constructing everything and anything. From factories to houses and roads. So, they're gonna need to make tens of thousands of bricks, heck maybe even hundreds of thousands of them. There's a lot of anticipation going through this town.

"Can't they just have bricks be delivered constantly?" she asked. Leadfoot didn't think she understood the seriousness of the situation.

"There just isn't any time for all of that," he answered. "They say they're already behind due to most of the summer being already gone. So, there's a group of about fifty of us, from all different walks of life, starting the process. Word has been sent out for more workers." He hesitated a bit then added, "The other part of the deal is that they are providing food and shelter for us guys that don't have it. We work on site, and we live on site. They have bunks set up for us inside, out of the weather. That's a big plus even though it gets hot in there and most of us will go out and sleep under the stars. They like to keep us close, so they know we'll be there to work in the morning." He added a chuckle.

"Sounds a little bit like slavery to me."

"Well, it sho' ain't," he answered gruffly. She noticed again that whenever Leadfoot got ticked off his accent comes out. "Anyone can leave whenever they want. We're just promised somethin' in return for our hard work. Not very many people doin' that these days."

Elizabeth could feel anxiety beginning to wash over her body. She could feel her sense of reality being sucked away from her down into a whirlpool. She felt like one of life's big struggles was arising in front of her. "So, you're saying you're leaving me? I thought we came to Harrisburg to see about finding a place for a fresh start."

Leadfoot never looked over to her. He just kept looking up at the loft that would be full of hay in a few weeks. "Oh, we'll be having a fresh start. I just don't think the fresh start is what you were expecting before we got here. Have faith, Tumbleweed, have faith." She wasn't exactly sure what he meant by that. But if there was one thing she knew about Leadfoot it was somewhere along the road that things always looked up. So, she grabbed her little wooden cross and said a little prayer to God to help her find a way out of an upcoming storm she knew was blowing in her path.

The rooster crowed before the bell rang today. Robert must have slept in a few minutes this morning. Anyway it was time to get to work. Elizabeth got out of the back of the wagon and walked to the milk barn where Robert was already milking the first cow. Elizabeth awkwardly stood around not quite sure what to say or what to do.

"Have you seen Leadfoot this morning?" she asked as she fumbled with her wooden cross in her hand.

Robert answered without missing a beat on milking the cow, "Saw him leave about a little over an hour ago but didn't talk to him. Not quite sure why he left. Do you know?"

So Robert didn't sleep in. "He found him a job. A good job that provides food and shelter. He'll be making and loading bricks. Eventually build things with them, I suppose. That's what he's really good at. I know," she said "I saw him continue a building project in Ohio."

"Shelter ain't all that good . . . it's just a tent," Robert said. "If it rains then they go to sleep in a sweltering warehouse. It'd be better to stay here. Plenty of work to do here."

"Leadfoot says it's too hard to trust the animals. They're too stubborn for their own good."

"Oh," said Robert. "I trust the four-legged animals way more than the two-legged ones. Humans are the ones that are hard to work with. You can anticipate what the four-legged ones will do. Leadfoot is a prime example. Everything was going good and then, out of nowhere, he's gone." Robert shook his head and mumbled to himself, "Didn't see that comin'." Elizabeth uncomfortably stood still not sure what to do as she watched Robert start to fret and fume. "If you're not gonna leave, too, then grab a bucket and a cow and get to milking. Do it just like yesterday as I showed you. Ellen will have breakfast ready by the time we're done milking. After you get your belly full then you can be on your own way."

Elizabeth was befuddled. "What? On my own way?"

"Yeah, you came with him, I assume that you'll leave with him."

Elizabeth could feel a storm of anxiety build within her gut, push up through her throat and rise to her cheeks. "I don't want to leave if I don't have to. I like it here, Mr. Wymer. Really, I do."

Robert was getting annoyed. "I'd rather you stay too, but you're gonna leave. Your kind of people always leave. You people . . . "

"You people?" Elizabeth was getting steamed. The more agitated Robert got, Elizabeth got just as riled.

Robert steeled his chin outwardly. "Yes, you people. You've been given an opportunity on this farm to better yourself by doing an honest day's work. Work that would lead to weeks, months, even years of being able to provide for yourselves and maybe even a family later on down the road." His voice was getting louder. Elizabeth wondered if Ellen could hear what was being said. "But you guys have this code, this . . . code for the road that says that you help each other along the road by looking for food in return for doing a little work. Then you're back on a train looking, I don't know . . . looking for another code or sign to see if this new location is a safe place or not. Well, dadgumit, Elizabeth, this could be a start of a life. A good life if you would stop moving and just look around. Look around and see what's about. There is everything here that you will ever need! But you won't." A frustrated Robert went back to milking. He yelled over his shoulder towards her, "So you might as well be on your way."

Ugh.

That comment.

That comment crushed.

The old Elizabeth would have walked over, knocked over his bucket, and kicked the stool out from under him. Then she would have given him the one finger wave and would have been out the door. But she was trying to become a more understanding and patient human being. Even though Robert's comment sounded like he had given up hope on her, she didn't want to let him down. So, she gathered herself, grabbed a stool and started milking. She wanted to show him that she was a dependable person and she almost kept up pace with him. Though she was slower than he was, she had much improved since the last time.

When the milking was finished, Robert washed up and went towards the house for breakfast expecting her to be behind him. He was surprised to find that she wasn't going to the house. Instead, she was loading up the milk bottles in the crates and putting them on the wagon. When that was done, she tended to the horse and prepared her to pull the wagon to town. Robert came out of the house and climbed into the seat. Elizabeth jumped up next to him, ready to go on the delivery route. Robert stared at her. He was shocked that she had the nerve to actually jump up and sit beside him.

"Wait, wait!" shouted Ellen as she came hurrying out of the house. She went over to Elizabeth's side of the wagon. "Here," she said as she handed her an egg sandwich. "You gotta eat to keep up your energy, and wow, do you ever have spirit!" Robert winked at Ellen as he let a smirk creep over his face. Elizabeth worked hard. She did just about everything right before Robert got to it. She seemed to be one step in front of him.

They got back to the farm after they finished the route. Like the day before and the day before that, there were chores to do. Always and always more chores to do. Robert told Elizabeth to come inside for lunch. And with a little of his coaxing, she agreed. After lunch, she stayed busy all the way up to supper. After supper, Elizabeth went to the barn and was fidgety. Although she wanted to stay, she wasn't sure if she was allowed. So just in case, she watered her mule and fed him. Then she hitched the beast to the wagon. Elizabeth was coaching herself in what to say once she got the courage to go up to the house and tell Robert and Ellen that she wanted to stay. If they would say no, then she would be ready to leave.

She heard someone clear their throat at the barn door. As she turned around, she saw Ellen standing there. "Come on over here and sit on this bale of hay, Elizabeth, I want to talk to you." They sat and then Ellen spoke, "When I look at you, you remind me of me when I was about your age. My mother gave birth to my older sister five years before I was born. She lost her life during my delivery. After her death, Father moved us into Muncie where he had bought an inn. There he did all the maintenance and all the accounting. My aunt, his sister, raised us and ran the kitchen and dining room. When my sister and I were old enough, we worked alongside both of them."

Ellen continued her story. "Our mother's death had made us grow up much faster than most kids our age. Father was a good man, but he had a strong taste for whiskey. One night after an afternoon of drinking in the local establishment, Father said that he and some friends were heading west to help build a railroad that would reach across the country. Basically, he was done trying to raise two mouthy teenage girls and wanted an adventure. That was the last time we ever saw him. Word had come back from out West saying that there were some men from Indiana that had gotten overrun by some Indians, but we weren't sure if Father was in that group. More than likely, he is buried in some unmarked grave. At least that's what I believe."

Elizabeth tried to hold her amazement in check, but she was in awe at the thought of Indians surging over the men and possibly ending their lives.

Ellen went on. "After a few years our aunt came down with a sickness that she just couldn't shake. My sister and I were thrust into running the inn. We hired a maintenance man to help out with the heavy work. Eventually he and my sister took a liking to each other." Ellen closed her eyes for a moment and sighed. Then she continued speaking. "I had never felt so out of place and alone in my life. Sure, my sister would always be there for me, but I felt that I now had to share her with her future husband.

Then one Saturday afternoon, a young man comes to the inn and asks if he could have lunch even though he didn't have a room. Normally, meals were only for customers of the inn. But he said that he hadn't eaten all day except for an apple, and he had a long train ride back home. He was cute so I thought I'd let him. Just as I was taking him to a table, I heard my sister scream. The man and I ran to see what was the matter. There was a cow tied up to the handrail post by the front steps of the inn."

"Oh, that's my dairy cow," the man said. "Her name is Clarabelle. I brought her down with me from Harrisburg by train. I took her to the trading center to see what I could get for her. No one was interested. So, I guess she'll go back home with me. She'll be alright out there."

"I couldn't get over the thought of being on a passenger train and seeing a man pulling a cow down the aisle, Ellen said."

"That man was Mr. Wymer, wasn't it?" Elizabeth smiled as she guessed. She could see a glimmer in Ellen's eye as she was telling the story.

"It was," she softly answered. "At that moment I knew I was going to marry that man. He was so kind to that animal. And especially kind to me. He proceeded to come to see me most Saturdays. Eventually he proposed, and we got married. The rest is history."

Elizabeth was happy to see her new friend was fortunate in finding love. But she was also a little confused. "Ellen, I don't understand why you told me that story." Ellen got up from the bale of hay and started to speak but was interrupted by Robert as he walked through the barn doors.

"First things first," he began, "I need to apologize to you for the way I acted this morning. You see, I knew Leadfoot wasn't going to be around much longer. I could tell this kind of work wasn't his cup of tea. The other day he told me that he had noticed how much you liked it here. He told me about you not having a family and that you were looking for a more stable place to be instead of riding the rails and living by the code for the road. You are one heck of a worker. He told me that you could be a tad stubborn and are not very fond of people telling you what to do. I think I saw a little of that this morning when I got you all steamed up in the britches . . . and I loved it. You see, we were never able to have any kids. And though the work that needs to be done around here is more suited to a male, you've sold me on the idea of you being able to do the work, and possibly even more."

Ellen stepped in to take over for Robert, "Elizabeth, this is a good place. It has so much to offer a young person. The work is hard, but the reward of that hard work is great. Elizabeth, would you like to stay with us? Not as a farmhand but as part of the family."

Elizabeth was wondering what was going on. The anxiety that she felt weighing over her for the last twenty-four hours was evaporating away. The feeling of a whirlpool that was sucking her life away was now cascading back to her with a calming force. She couldn't understand why these tears were falling down her face. She wasn't sad. These must be those tears of joy that she'd heard of a time or two. And she loved them.

Ellen reached out to Elizabeth and placed something in her hand. "It is a chain from an old necklace. I thought that if it was okay with you, Robert could drill a small hole in your cross. Then you could wear it as a necklace. That way you won't lose it by carrying it in your pocket." Elizabeth reached out and hugged Ellen.

"So, is this what a mother's love is supposed to feel like?" was all that Elizabeth could think about as she broke down and cried. She cried tears of joy.

"Wait," Elizabeth pulled away from Ellen and wiped tear trails from her cheeks. "What about Leadfoot?"

"What about him?" asked Robert.

Elizabeth didn't know how to finish what she wanted to say. "Uh, I don't know. Um, is he staying here? I mean, where is he? Will he, uh, can he come back here?"

Robert answered, "Relax, Elizabeth, he will always be welcome here. He's a part of your life and we understand that. But for the moment he has to stay with the brick company until something else comes up. You are more than welcome to go see him whenever. But consider this your home. Your own room, your own space . . . everything."

For the rest of the summer, Elizabeth worked hard. From early morning until late in the evening. And she loved it. She found the stability that she had craved. One of the biggest changes was not having to carry her bindle stick with her at all times, though she always left it under her bed along with the cleaver Papa Gio had given her. It left Ellen with an uneasy feeling when she saw it, but after some of the stories that Elizabeth had told Robert and Ellen, they completely understood and allowed her to keep them near her.

Rain and more rain, he thought. Today was the only day that it hadn't rained in a week. I guess man demands that his crops grow. So, the gods relent and supply man with all he can handle. The well-worn Stetson that this man wore stayed damp throughout the early morning and had a tough time drying out in this humid air. He's not sure where he pilfered the Stetson. He thought only cowboys out West wore those. He hadn't seen any cowboys and he had never been out West. Frankly, this is the farthest west he'd been. He spent most of his time back east working various jobs from day to day. He liked them all, and yet despised every one he had.

"Here you are, Partner," the driver/owner of the wagon drawled as he slowed down his two horses that were pulling the wagon. "This here is the place I was telling you about. This side is Jonesboro and that town across the river is Harrisburg."

Once the horse drawn wagon came to a final stop, the traveler climbed out the back of the open wagon. He had spent the last three days with the driver on this wagon. He started out the trip by sitting up on the box seat with him, but the incessant drivel coming from him led the traveler to go back on the open wagon for some peace and quiet with the driver's dog and the boxes of freight that the driver had picked up.

The traveler had been walking the road when he ran into this man with the horses and wagon. He'd been walking because it wasn't safe for him to be hitching rides on trains just now. Rumor had it that a bear of a man had thrown two train bulls off a moving train when they tried to send him flying out of the railcar. Their clubs were useless against the man as he pushed through the assault on him and threw the bulls out of the opening and down a steep hill. He was a hero to a railcar of about a dozen hobos for the duration of the ride until an unexpected stop in a nearby town led to several sleeping hobos being beaten badly by local policemen. The ones that didn't escape were jailed and eventually ended up giving information against the "bear of a man" and the earlier events of that night. But he had jumped off the train just before they entered the town, and he was never caught for his wrongdoings. So, he thought it would be best if he stayed off trains for the foreseeable future.

The traveler jumped down to the ground. He pulled his Stetson off, set it on the back of the wagon, ran his hands over his face, and pulled his long greasy hair back from his face and ears. He put his hat back on and looked around to decide his next move.

"Remember our agreement?" The unremitting driver said. "Half payment to begin the ride, the other half upon reaching the destination. This is it." Then he stuck out a well-worn palm to receive the final payment.

The traveler couldn't believe the gall of this man. He looked around to see how many people were watching. He thought for a moment about slashing the driver's throat and throwing him off the wagon and down to the river. *Does he even know the things that I've done since I've been in this country?*

"I suppose you'll want to make camp down there near the river." The driver offered as he pointed to the Harrisburg side. "What is it you guys call it. . . hobo jungle, right?" The traveler decided against killing this man. He didn't want to start the day off in a bad way. *It's hard to sleep off the evil you do if it's done in the morning.* The traveler reached deep into his pocket and pulled out a dollar gold piece and placed it into the driver's palm.

"I am no hobo," the traveler growled as he gave the driver a most menacing gaze. He was daring the driver to ask for more payment. That would give the traveler a reason to make the driver's mouth shut up forever. The driver was almost looking the traveler eye to eye from his seat on the wagon. That alone, should have left the driver in awe. And yet, the crusty driver was no buffoon and proved to know when enough was enough. He placed the coin in his pants pocket and nodded to the traveler and was on his way back to where he came from without even a word.

The traveler turned away from the departing wagon and towards the decisions that were ahead of him. He decided to go across the rickety bridge and see what was in store in this boomtown. The sky was clearing of clouds. Hopefully by noon the rain clouds will be burned away by the sun. This was a good sign. Even a good sign for a bear of a man from Russia named Nikita.

18

The trip across the bridge was a quick walk. The bridge was made from very thick rope and strong wood boards. It tended to sway a bit due to the constant motion of wagons and people crossing back and forth into both towns. Nikita reached the Harrisburg side of the river and was trying to decide his next move. He was hungry, but his meager rations consisted of two crab apples which was barely a morsel for a big man like Nikita. He also needed a bath, but then again, most people always needed a bath.

As he was trying to decide what his next move would be, a breeze wafted the aroma of recently distinguished campfires to his nose. That meant food. Or at least the possibility of leftovers. It was a short walk to where the campfires were located. They could be spotted just to the south of the bridge along the river. The greasy smell of the campfire smoke made the walk hopeful that the slight trek would be prosperous. He kept his eyes glued to the smoke that was emanating from a prospective site. Once he got there, he closely inspected the area and didn't see anyone. *Looks like someone hasn't been gone too long,* he thought as he slid his blade from its sheath. The blade was a thick one. It could be used for all sorts of good and has been used for all sorts of bad. He took the blade and scooped through the ashes, looking for clues on what was recently cooked. He found some scrapped eggshells. Hopefully that meant some bacon or sausage also. His mouth watered just at the thought of it.

"Hey, what are you doing?" came a voice from the tree line at the river. "There's nothing there in that camp for you." Nikita had his back to the river and to the approaching voice. He cursed quietly to himself for that error as he gripped the handle of the knife. The man from the river slowly approached Nikita with great caution. As he was getting closer, he was beginning to see that he was dealing with a very large man. "Slowly turn around and face me . . . and drop that blade while you are at it." Nikita slowly turned around as directed but didn't drop the knife.

"You don't tink I give you advantage by dropping de blade, do you?" Nikita tried to hide his Russian accent. He didn't like talking too much to anyone. He had quickly learned that most English speaking people thought of him as a dunce when he spoke. It frustrated him because almost no one that he dealt with could speak Russian.

"Ah, Russian, eh?" The man said. He didn't get much closer to Nikita. His size and the look in his eyes told him just about everything he needed to know. The main cue was to stay back. The man didn't live this long by sticking his neck out and leaving it exposed.

"Is Russian good ting or bad ting for you?" Nikita scanned the other campsites to see if anyone was watching or not. He didn't see anyone paying attention to them at that time. His grip on the blade handle tightened. The man didn't know, but his next answer was going to decide if he lived or died.

"Heck, I don't care what you are. We're all God's children. I'm just surprised. We haven't had any Russians here until recently.

Lately, there's been a few passing through. I'm hearing most are traveling to the north or way out west. The heat and humidity here in the Midwest don't particularly mesh with you candle eaters. Why, I bet . . . " The next sentence was cut off with the blade to the man's throat. The large but swift Nikita rushed the man. His weight and momentum pushed the man back up against a tree.

"Do. Not. Call. Me. Candle eater. If you do you veel never take breath again." The man wanted to look up to Nikita's face, but Nikita was too tall and, frankly, he was afraid that the blade would slice through his neck if he moved an inch. The man swore that the blade had sliced the skin on his throat, and he was probably right. All he could do was wait for Nikita's mercy or for him to viciously finish him off. Luckily, mercy was shown, but maybe not the next time. Nikita pulled away from the man and kept scanning the area for onlookers as he walked back to the smoldering cook fire. Satisfied that there were none he, Nikita leaned on a stump with a booted foot. He rested the blade on that bended knee, ever ready for quick use if needed. The man stood and watched Nikita saunter away from him and grabbed his neck. He didn't see any blood on his hand when he looked at it, but he was sure that the blade left a mark. "So how duss a man get someting to eat in dis town?" It's funny how men like Nikita can ask a question, but in reality, it's a direct statement or demand.

"That all depends," answered the man as he kept his distance from Nikita. "If you have money you can go up the hill into town. There's a small general store. The three saloons each have free salted meats available, but the catch there is that you have to pay for the beer or whiskey." Beer and whiskey sounded good. *Man, what I'd do for some back home homemade vodka,* Nikita thought. But he stayed silent waiting for the man to come up with another option. "Of course," the man stammered, "if I had any extra, I would share. Uh, you know, be neighborly and all. But all I have left is what I'll eat tonight. I work in that new glass factory there. I'm fairly new to town and I work nights at the glass factory. I picked up an extra job at the lumber mill for extra pay and that's where I'm going in a little bit. I'm one paycheck away to renting me a real place to stay instead of the old tent and all." Nikita looked around. The man was right. The only thing that was keeping the tent together was the dried mud and mold. He wasn't getting the answer that he wanted. He wondered if he was going to have to use force to get it. He didn't really want to. Using force made a man hungrier than he already was. "Um, I guess if you had something to trade, I'd be willing to go without supper tonight." The man was walking on thin ice, and he knew it. "I could possibly do without supper for the Stetson you have there. Heck, I'd go without supper and breakfast for that." Nikita stood up from the stump to make himself look more intimidating.

"Dee last owner of hat loved dis hat. But not love it enough to keep hees head to go wit it," Nikita explained as he slowly ran his index finger across his throat and jugular veins to make the point extremely clear. The man got the point. He got so much of the point that he gave Nikita the food. He even warmed it up over the fading coals. Nikita looked up from his food to see the man leaning against a tree looking at a pocket watch. "You have place to go?" The man looked up at him.

"Yeah, I have to get to work. My extra job starts in about forty-five minutes." He hoped that Nikita took the hint and would leave . . . forever. But if Nikita did, then he didn't acknowledge it.

"So, go. I do not need sitting like babe." Nikita stood and stretched which made him look even more menacing along with the loudest growl of a yawn. He walked over to the tent. "Time for nap and stretch out bones. You go. When you come back, maybe I be here, maybe no." He stretched out on the man's bedroll, faced the man, and closed his eyes. The man thought about not coming back to this place . . . ever again. "By de way," Nikita spoke with his eyes closed, "I do like dat pocket watch. Veddy, veddy much. It is shiny." Something told the man that if he came back here later in the day, the pocket watch would be lost or the hand that held it would be gone.

It was a long nap. Nikita didn't like taking long naps or getting a full night's sleep. It made him feel that he didn't have control of what was going on around him. Perhaps it was a guilty conscience. Keeping control of situations had always been an essential part to his survival. Maybe it was past bad experiences. Lord knows that he had enough contemptible baggage following him around. He sat up from the man's bedroll and looked around. *Oh my,* he thought, *it gotten late.* The sun had not set, but it was sliding behind the woods which encompassed both sides of the river. It was getting dark, but it was light enough for him to look over at a couple of occupied campsites. The men there were staring at Nikita. It was as if they saw a monster. Never had they seen such an intimidating figure. Nikita looked around for any evidence that the man had been back while he slept. Satisfied that there was no such indication, he went back into the tent and searched through his belongings for money. Nikita had his own money but didn't feel compelled to use it if he could utilize another's. Having found none, the frustrated Russian bear decided to not make a scene by going over to one of the other campsites and asking for food or money. He left and walked up the hill towards town. He remembered the man telling him that there were saloons that offered salted meats with the purchase of beer or whiskey. He hadn't gotten used to the bitter taste of beer, but he did have an inclination for this country's whisky. So off he went.

19

It was a quick jaunt to the saloons once he walked up the hill into Harrisburg. Nestled right on Main Street and a stone's throw from the train station sat the Shooting Star Saloon and Losure's Landing and Livery. The location of these drinking establishments was conveniently placed where any worker heading to or from one of the new factories had to walk past these businesses. Nikita tried to decide which one he'd go to. He chose Losure's Landing and Livery to go to first. *Great choice I make,* he said to himself. The owner had thought of it all. Saloon on the main floor, sleeping rooms upstairs and a livery stable out back. Nikita thought that the place would be expensive. But soon realized that it wasn't. He found the free lunch table. He grabbed a handful of cold cuts and went to one of the tables and sat down to eat his first handful. People stared at him as he sat there. When he was done, he went back for seconds. Nikita got to the free lunch table and was getting a handful of cheese and pretzels when a burly man wearing overalls went over to him and told him that the tables were for paying customers.

"You'll have to stand at the bar if you're going to eat at the freeloader table with the other hobos," was all he said. Nikita chewed up the pretzels and blew them into the man's face. As he wiped the salted food off his mouth, Nikita slammed a fist to the overall wearing man's jaw, knocking him out before he landed on the floor.

"I am not hobo," Nikita said and then stuffed the cheese into his mouth and thought he better leave before a crowd formed around him. So off he went to check out the Shooting Star Saloon. He wasn't sure that he liked this place. *Dis place es gloomy and dark.* Thought Nikita. *Like me.* He walked up to the bar and asked the bartender where the free meat table was located. The barkeep quickly explained that he had to buy something to drink first before he could eat from the free lunch table. Though Nikita didn't like the answer, he was thirsty and decided to buy a bottle of whisky. The barkeep gave him a bottle and a shot glass and directed him to the free lunch table.

This table was awful. There were many choices of meats. There were also many flies swarming around the meats and cheeses. Nikita picked through the meats and took what looked edible. There wasn't much. Thank God for the cheese. The cheese was covered in a layer of green mold. Not appetizing yet fit for consumption. Nikita scraped the fuzzy mold off the cheese with his teeth and spat it on the floor. The barkeep saw Nikita spitting it on the floor but didn't say anything. He turned away. Pick your battles. Nikita poured himself a shot and threw it to the back of his throat. He was pouring himself another as he swallowed the first. He repeated this act frequently for the next half hour as he stood shoulder to shoulder with the other drunks, all of them guarding their drinks and rotten food like a lion preventing the hyenas from taking his prey.

Nikita had about half of the whiskey drained. He turned around and leaned on the bar with the shot glass and bottle in hand. He scanned the small crowd of people looking through his blood shot eyes. Every soul in the saloon had the same attire and wore the same expression on their face. Everyone looked familiar and yet everyone was a stranger. Except that guy. That guy sitting with another man. Both of them were tearing into their own turkey leg. The familiar looking guy locked eyes on Nikita as he teetered his way to their table. He pulled out a chair from their table and plopped down in it as he rested his feet on the other empty chair.

"Hey," said the unfamiliar man, "these tables are for people that have paid for a meal. Get lost!" The words were spoken without any eye contact whatsoever. Nikita looked over to the familiar man for consent as the man was staring at Nikita bug eyed over his own turkey leg.

"I guess it's okay until the barkeep says he has to go," said the familiar man as he picked turkey gristle from his teeth with dirty fingers. "Have yourself a good nap on my bedroll, did ya?" The familiar man asked with as much gusto as he could spare, which wasn't much. Nikita didn't answer, but the familiar man seemed to acknowledge Nikita and that was a start.

Nikita directed his conversation to the familiar man from the campsite but kept an eye on the man he didn't know. "Today you say to me of jobs to work in town. Who es job boss or es middleman for me to talk to?" Neither man answered, but they kept looking at each other as if they were waiting on one another to speak up. After a couple of moments, Nikita poured himself a shot. He threw it back and slammed the glass on the barrel table. It sounded like a gunshot. Almost everyone got quiet. "BRING ME TWO SHOT GLASS!" Nikita bellowed. The barkeep hastily did what was asked and scurried away. Nikita poured each man a shot out of his own bottle. As the men downed their drinks, Nikita reached over and grabbed both greasy turkey legs from the men. *Just like take candy from babe,* thought Nikita. He took a big bite from each one and rudely spoke with his mouth full. "Now, dat you hear me, give me answer or I eat all de meat and den I keel you boat vit de leg bone. Veddy easy ting to do," as he took another bite of the turkey. Turkey grease soaking into his mustache and beard.

"C'mon, Yeager, give him his answer, will ya. I'm hungry and that's all I'll have to eat for the rest of the night." The unfamiliar man yearned for his turkey leg that was in Nikita's hand. Nikita's English was getting better with practice, but his tone was always brusque. He tried a smile, but that only made him seem more psychotic.

"Dah, Yeager, nice German name. Meester Yeager, who do I talk to for job?" Nikita poured them both another shot and then immediately another. The alcohol loosened them up a bit. Yeager proceeded to give tips about whom to talk to for employment. There were plenty of jobs to be had. After the bottle was empty, Nikita barked for another one to be brought to him. He even bought a round of turkey legs for all three of them.

They finished their greasy turkey legs and were also feeling quite inebriated from the whiskey. "Oh my. I have to be on my way," slurred Yeager. "I have to be at work in an hour."

The other man agreed that it was time for him to catch some shut eye. "I must leave as well. I have to load tons of bricks tomorrow and have them delivered to job sites all around town. Man, am I gonna feel that whiskey tomorrow."

Nikita laughed to himself then teased, "I will seet here and finish de viskey. Who know what den? Maybe I go back to my campsite and sleep tonight."

Yeager cocked his chin towards Nikita. "Your campsite?" The disgust couldn't be disguised in Yeager's tone of voice. Nikita stared back at him and raised his bottle to his lips and drank from it. He never took his leer off the man who had just realized that he'd lost his tent and belongings. Then Nikita bellowed a belch that sounded more like a roar from a bear. Yeager really didn't like this man at all, but he was smart enough to know that he couldn't handle Nikita one on one . . . just barely smart enough.

Yeager and the other man got up to leave Nikita alone at the table without speaking a word to him. They didn't think there was a need for any parting pleasantries and had hoped that they would not see him for a long time, if ever again. After they left, Nikita sat by himself observing the patrons and workers until a small squabble arose on the other side of the saloon. The barkeep gave him a dour look as he went over to put a stop to the fight. Nikita raised his hands up as if to concede defeat. This was one fight that the Russian Bear had no part with. As the participants of the squabble were being let out the side door of the saloon to take their fight elsewhere, Nikita got up and went over to their upturned table and chairs. Under the table was broken glass from a couple shot glasses and a still half full bottle of rot gut whiskey laying on its side. Nikita picked up the half full bottle and decided it was worth taking. He walked out the front door and out onto the boardwalk. As he started to cross the street, he saw Yeager and his friend intently talking in the shadows of a nearby building. They were huddled close to each other. Nikita could make out Yeager stealing glances over his shoulder as a couple of workers passed by. He couldn't hear a word that they were saying, but he would bet a bottle of whiskey that they were talking about him. Why else would they be talking in such a way in the dark of night.

Nikita returned to the campsite. He thought about just going to sleep, but he really wasn't tired since he had such a long nap earlier. He decided it would be best to have a small fire. A little light might be beneficial so he could see if he received any unwanted guests. He grabbed the wood that Yeager had gotten earlier today and started a small fire. He sprinkled twigs around the back and sides of the tent. That way if someone stepped on them while he was sleeping, he would hear them snap and break.

After an hour or so, most of the other campfires had been extinguished as everyone went to sleep. He could hear a harmonica playing a mournful song farther down from his campsite. His site was the nearest one to the bridge. The moon was very bright that night and he could see the basic shape of the bridge rather easily. It wasn't used much at this time of night. He was thinking about putting his fire out, when he thought he saw a small reddish orange glow. The light of the moon helped him see that it was the lit end of a cigar. He then could see the shape of a man on the other end of the cigar. He looked to be carrying a fishing pole and heading towards the bridge. The man must've been going to fish for catfish. Nikita thought fishing sounded interesting . . . or at least taking someone's fish sounded appealing.

He waited for about a half hour and then decided to go over the bridge and see what was up. He didn't want to sneak up on the fisherman and startle him particularly for his own safety if the man was armed and had an itchy finger. It was too dark to see any detailed footing, so the element of surprise was completely gone. Nikita could smell the cigar and knew that the fisherman wasn't that far away. Lo and behold, there he was. He was under the bridge sitting on the rocky ground leaning against the far end of a fallen dead tree. Nikita could only see the pole, the cigar and the man's legs.

"Hallo," said Nikita, keeping his distance for the fisherman's safety and his, "I vill stay away. I do not bother you. I vant to vatch how you catch fish. I never catch fish. I never had luck." The man didn't move an inch nor acknowledged Nikita.

"You definitely don't have much luck. In fact, what luck you had has just done ran out," said a voice coming from behind Nikita. The man had come up the trail from the river. For a quick moment, Nikita was startled. Then he heard the click of the hammer pulled back on a gun. The fisherman laid his pole down and got up and walked over towards Nikita. The fisherman was Yeager. The cigar was between his teeth and instead of carrying a pole as he walked towards Nikita, he was wielding a filet knife. He just smiled. He had Nikita. Nikita put his hands up in surrender. The gun wielding man was Yeager's friend from the saloon. "We figured that if you had money to blow for buying rounds of whiskey and turkey legs, then you should have plenty more stashed on your person."

"And the rest of my money that I had stashed in the tent," added Yeager.

Nikita was confused but made a mental note of possible stashed money in the tent, "I don't have your stash money. I know nothing about stash." He still had his hands in the air, but not as high. Nikita noticed that Yeager had moved out of the shooting line and closer to the river. Nikita kept an eye on Yeager, but he was more concerned with the gun handler.

"Any last words you want to come stumbling out of your mouth, you ratbag?" The man asked as he pointed the gun at Nikita's head?

Nikita acted confused. "I not know vhy you call me dat. Vhy you angry to me? I not know you." Nikita then steeled his eyes at the man. "I hope you to know dat when you shoot gun, eet make loud sound. Eet wake people and dey come see what es happen. Den dey vill come geet you."

Nikita gritted his teeth and with a sneer said, "Shoot me, cowboy. Shoot me dead." The man hesitated for a moment as he stared into Nikita's evil eyes. This was the pause that Nikita needed. He swiftly reached to the back of his Stetson where he had two six inch daggers hidden inside the brim and with professional precision he flung the daggers at the man. One dagger hit him in the left eye, the other split his bottom lip, chipped a tooth and then the dagger thudded onto the beaten down dirt.

The man never got off a shot. Nikita was on him instantly as the man crumbled to the ground dead as a doornail. "Ugh," grumbled Nikita to himself, "I need practice more. Only one blade sticked." He grabbed the gun and spun around towards Yeager. He was still in the same spot trying to figure out what had just happened. The plan that the two men came up with was for Yeager to wait until the gunshot and then blitz Nikita and stab him in the chest just to make sure he was dead.

After Nikita was dead, Yeager had secretly thought that he'd then run over to his friend and stab him also and then get away before anyone showed up. He figured that a dead man couldn't give him up to the marshal. But since there was no shot, there stood Yeager, totally dumbfounded. He had to think quickly. He could feel the ticking of his life's clock slowly fading away.

"Now, remember what you just said to that dead man there," said Yeager. "You shoot that gun, and everyone will come a runnin'. It'll echo down in this riverbed under this here bridge." Yeager's eyes were scanning everywhere for an escape route. If he could keep yapping, maybe he could talk some sense into the bear. "Why, I'd bet that gun would sound like a cannon going off," he exaggerated. Nikita let the stammering continue because he already knew how this would end. It was quite humorous listening to Yeager with his arms flailing around emphasizing how he should be left to live. But both of them knew Yeager was going to die. Nikita couldn't allow him to live. He walked around the dead man so he could keep an eye on Yeager just in case he decided to do something stupid, like rush him while Nikita was crouched down over the dead man.

He searched the pockets for money or anything of value. The only things he found were a few small coins, and a key with a number on it. *Must be a hotel key,* Nikita thought. He thought for a moment that staying in the room may be an option, but only if he could get into a back door. People may realize that the occupant of the room would have been this dead man. He may check it out though. The whole time Nikita was shaking down the dead man, Yeager kept yapping and yapping. Nikita wasn't giving him much attention but snuck a few glances at him to be sure he wasn't doing anything that would hurt him.

Then he heard it. He heard the word that stuck in his soul deeper than any sword. Hobo. "Go to hell!! You're nothing but a filthy, loathsome, low life hobo," spat Yeager. Those would be the last words he spoke in this life. From a squatting position, Nikita flung the dagger that had missed its mark at Yeager. This time it was fruitful by landing just below the jaw in his neck. Yeager fell clutching the knife as if to pull it out of his neck. Nikita quickly went over and straddled him.

"I am no hobo," growled Nikita at the dying man. He then grabbed the filet knife off the ground where Yeager had dropped it. Nikita was about to use Yeager's own knife on him to put him out of his misery, but Yeager quickly bled out. Nikita searched the body for anything of value, but only found a few more coins than what the other man had on him, but hey, it was something. The last pocket he searched, though, was very profitable and made Nikita smile. The pocket watch that he saw earlier when he met Yeager. Nikita left the bodies right where they were. There was no use in moving them. They would be found as soon as the sun came up.

He did walk over to the spot where Yeager had been fishing. Nikita was hoping for a caught fish to take, but there was nothing but a drowned worm on the end of the hook. He got up and trudged through the dark back to Yeager's tent. As he approached it, Nikita surveyed the site to see if anyone was there or if anything looked awry. Everything looked normal, and he entered the tent. He searched the small area inside. There wasn't much area to hide anything let alone a stash of money. He looked under the cot and between the dirty blankets. He also searched a couple of locked boxes that were easily jimmied with a knife to find nothing of value. He sat on the side of the cot thinking that he was sure Yeager had said that there was a stash of money in his tent. He was sure that he searched everywhere in the tent and was confident that he hadn't left any stone unturned.

Except for that stone in the corner. Nikita went over to it and dropped on his knees. The stone was sunk down in the ground, but it was effortlessly plucked from the dirt. Under the stone was a tobacco tin. It was heavy in weight. Heavier than it should be even if it was still full of tobacco. He pulled it out of its hiding place and rested it on the ground. He then twisted off the cylindrical tin lid and dumped the contents out. What spilled out was a lot of coins! Silver and gold coins and newly printed paper money. There was even a stock certificate for shares for a railroad company. He wasn't sure what the certificate was meant for, but it must've been important if Yeager saved it with the money.

Nikita looked around the tent to see if there was anything of value left to take. After deciding there wasn't, he put all the coins and bills in his pockets. He started to fill up a pillowcase with his newfound valuables but decided against it because he thought that it would make him look like a hobo. Lord knows he despised hobos. He thought about torching the tent as he left, but decided against it. It wouldn't serve any real purpose. People will find the dead men soon enough. So, he went back into town with his loaded down coat in search of a back door of the hotel.

Nikita made it back into town with no trouble at all. No one was out and most people were asleep. He reached Losure's Landing and Livery but fretted about going in there on account of the earlier altercation that he had gotten into with the man wearing overalls. So instead of barreling into the establishment, he tried his best to sneak in and act like he was supposed to be there. He remembered that the staircase that led to the long landing of rooms was just to the left of the front door. He took the staircase, trying to act like he'd been there before.

It was quiet up there. He had a breath-taking view from the landing. He could see the whole saloon and bar. He turned around to see a full-length window. It took up most of the wall. It was still dark out so he couldn't see the landscape. He pulled the key out of his front pocket. It had a number eight on it.

The room was clear down at the end of the hallway. Nikita stepped off the landing and climbed the couple of steps to the hallway. Once he reached the room he decided he liked where it was. *Nice and quiet* he thought. He put the key in and turned the lock. The door sprang open. He stood there for a minute expecting someone to yell or come towards him. When no one did, he stepped in and closed the door behind him.

The only light in the room was coming from the moon through the window. He walked over to the desk and found an oil lamp. After he got it lit, he looked around the room. He found a couple of suitcases and a violin case. *Ah, Yeager's friend was a musician.* He sat on the bed and opened it up. It was empty except for some clothing. Nikita thought that he could use it as a case to keep some of his belongings.

Man, dis bed es comfortable. Ven vas last time I sleep on bed dis good? He laid across the bed for a moment to enjoy the softness of it. He would just rest his eyes for a moment or two. Then he would have to leave. He didn't feel that it was safe to stay for the rest of the night in the room.

One yawn led to another.

Then another.

Another.

A rooster crowed. Nikita bolted straight up on the bed. *Oh no. What time es eet?* He remembered he had Yeager's pocket watch. He looked at it. Almost 6:30 in the morning. Surely a fisherman had discovered the bodies by now. Nikita got up and rummaged through the rest of Yeager's friend's belongings. Not much was found of value except for a small razor to shave with and a few more coins. He looked around for a violin but didn't find one. He walked over to the desk and found a wash bowl with water in it. He cleaned himself up the best that he could and decided to go downstairs and take a chance on getting some breakfast. He thought it would be nice to sit at one of the tables and order real food.

He left the room and walked down the hallway. When he passed one of the rooms before the landing, a red-haired woman was sneaking out of another room. She was quietly closing the door when she saw Nikita. She gasped at the size of the man. She had never seen such a big man. She quickly passed him and gave him a wink. He made a mental note to find her for some company one of these nights.

He got to the landing, and what an impressive sight! Through the wall length window, he could see the expansion of the town growing eastward. The buildings were at different rates of completion. There were people going about their daily lives. Beyond the hustle and bustle was a wonderful sunrise coming up over the trees making the sky pop with oranges, pinks and reds that were pushing the deep blues high up into the sky. He found it interesting that the window on the landing showed the present as well as a view of what the future held for the town and its people.

He turned and walked down the rest of the staircase and found an unoccupied table in the back of the saloon. A man that Nikita thought may have been the owner was talking to a waitress as they both stared at him. He wore a short flat top and had long sideburns and a bushy mustache. The mustache reminded Nikita of a cousin of his back in the motherland. Eventually the man came up to Nikita.

"Good morning to you, sir. I am Mr. Losure, the proprietor of this establishment. The tables are for paying customers . . . " BAM! Nikita slammed down a small stack of silver coins, but big enough to pay for whatever he could eat. Mr Losure looked at the stack of coins in amazement. He then went to warn the cook of a huge breakfast order coming his way.

And boy was it ever a big order. Ham and cheese, grits, eggs, a big stack of bacon, hot cakes fresh out of the skillet. Nikita finished it with biscuits and gravy and toasted bread with strawberry jam. He washed it down with a tall glass of milk and a full pot of coffee.

As he was finishing up eating his meal fit for a bear, he overheard a couple men at the next table talking about needing employees to help lay bricks for a couple of new projects on the far east side of town. Nikita thought that one of these jobs may help him pass the time while he was in this town. He got up and went over to their table and asked about a job. They were both eager to employ him on the spot but suggested that he go up to his room and clean up and then come to the site and make it official. They left the saloon and Nikita went back to his table to finish his coffee.

"Excuse me," Mr. Losure said, "I didn't mean to eavesdrop into your conversation, but I couldn't help overhearing what the two gentlemen had said. I'm going to assume that you don't have a room here. I am the proprietor of this establishment and don't remember seeing you here before."

Nikita sat there thinking about how he was going to play this out. *People tink honesty es dee best policy, but eet's just the safe policy.* "I am to meet friend here in town," Nikita explained as he picked bacon gristle from his teeth. "I went up to de landing window and looked out to see if he es near. I come down to eat and wait for heem." Before Mr. Losure could say anything, Nikita added, "I may want room for de week. How much would eet be?"

Mr. Losure walked over next to the bar where he had a shotgun hidden. It was always good to have one within arm's length in case a situation got out of hand. He cleared his throat and was about to tell him, no. Then he saw silver coins that Nikita was re-stacking. He was willing to bet that there were more of them close by. "You may be in luck, sir. There was a room vacated last night by a man from St. Louis. You may have it for $5.95. That is our weekly rate." Normally Nikita would have strong armed the man into charging half of what was offered, but he thought against it. Nikita was pushing his luck for being here in the first place. Besides, he had a good sense about people and his gut told him that Mr. Losure knew how to use that shotgun if the situation was to get a little dicey.

Nikita went up to his room which was directly across from the room he stayed in last night. He placed his things on the floor next to the desk and cleaned himself up the best that he could. He decided that it may be good to find the barber shop and get a haircut. He may even be able to learn some local gossip, that is, had anyone found the bodies of Yeager and his friend? He was directed to head east up Main Street for a couple of blocks where Max's Barber Shop was located. Nikita walked in and looked around the small shop. Small shop, but big business. There was one barber, presumably Max, and four customers in the establishment.

"Good morning, sir," welcomed Max, "don't mind all these guys. I only have one other customer ahead of you. All these others are gabbing about the news in town." That got his attention. He tried to act indifferent as he listened in on the conversation, but quickly realized that the news was only that a local dairy farmer was expanding to the other side of town. Nikita was disappointed as he got into the barber chair when it was his turn. No one had found the bodies yet. Everyone left and it was just the barber and Nikita. "So, you're new around here, huh? How long have you been here? There's a lot of new people coming to town because of the factories and all. Are you here for one of those jobs?" Quizzed Max. Nikita wasn't sure how to respond to the barrage of questions from Max. But he knew he didn't want to give too much information out about himself.

"I am here for factory job." Nikita's heavy Russian accent came through. He felt the barber's hands hesitate when he heard his voice. After a few minutes the hair was lightly trimmed, but still long and bushy. Then Max began trimming the beard.

"So, did you come to town on the train?" Max could feel Nikita tense up at the question and he could feel his deadening stare. He did not appreciate the question presuming/indicating that he arrived as a hobo. Before he could answer, a customer opened the shop door and sat to wait his turn.

"So have you heard the big news today?" Asked the waiting customer.

"Yeah," responded Max as he kept trimming Nikita's beard. "Old Wymer is expanding his dairy farm clear out near Walnut Creek. There's a lot more room out there than where he's at on Kokomo Road. It may seem that he's way out there on the creek, but give it time, things are expanding that way rather quickly."

"No, not THAT big news," replied the customer, "the news that just happened about an hour ago. Two bodies were found dead! And I'm not talking heart attack dead! I'm talking murdered dead!" Even though Nikita was expecting to hear the news soon, it still caught him off guard. He swallowed hard and just about made the barber cut his neck.

"Careful, fella," Max warned, "this isn't the time to get all flinchy. Another move like that may result in a bloodletting."

Nikita slowly spoke, "Den your blood would meex wit mine on de floor." Max tried to ignore the comment and continued trimming the beard. He wanted this guy out of his chair.

The waiting customer resumed the current rumor. "Yeah, I guess both men were stabbed, rather brutally. No one seems to know either guy. There's no way to identify either one of them. Word is that they are probably a couple of filthy hobos that piggy backed on a train into town. They were found under the bridge near the hobo campsites." Max the barber stole a quick glance at Nikita for some type of reaction because he wondered if this guy could be involved. Nikita didn't give any. He just stared over the top of Max's head as the barber finished trimming the beard.

Max finished up the cut and told him he was done. Nikita didn't wait for the barber to take off the cape. He ripped it off and got up, put his Stetson back on and walked to the door. "That'd be ten cents, sir, for the beard trim and haircut. I know it's not much, but it's all I charge." The barber's attempt of a joke fell short of being funny to Nikita.

Nikita stood at the door for a moment and then turned to the barber and tossed him a silver coin and growled, "Keep de change. I am no hobo." Then he left the barber shop and went to look for employment.

Nikita found the two men that he had met earlier at the saloon at one of the work sites that they had talked about. The two men were brothers and owned a construction company and were having a hard time getting the correct supplies to the right sites. The last guy that had overseen the distribution of materials did not have the respect of his workers. They were stealing the company blind.

They both loved the idea of Nikita managing and overseeing materials. They were sure that his formidable disposition would result in nothing short of near perfect results. There'd be almost no way someone would steal from the company under Nikita's reign. He was even given his own horse to ride between construction sites. Nikita laughed at how much this really made him look like a cowboy even though he had never ridden a horse. Mr. Losure would give him pointers on how to control the animal when he went to the livery to pick up the horse. Nikita talked Mr. Losure into taking the horse out into the country to help him practice. He quickly learned how to understand the animal, or maybe the horse was a quick learner how to deal with the Russian. After a few hours, he looked like a seasoned veteran up on the horse and quickly added this to his persona to "win" his workers' respect and trust.

. . . Except for one poor soul. A couple of days in his new job, Nikita had caught one of the workers hiding nails under a nearby bush. He learned that the man had pilfered some wood and a hammer and handsaw. He was to build a shack on some land that he'd purchased on the outskirts of town. Nikita allowed the man to keep all that he had stolen. A few of the other workers were completely surprised at his actions until they saw the man the next day. The man had all his fingers crushed, presumably by the hammer he'd taken. He also walked with a severe limp that wasn't there before. So, the worker got to keep his bounty, but lost his job . . . and the use of his hands and legs for the foreseeable future. The shack would not be built anytime soon.

The next two months were smooth sailing. Nothing was stolen, not a splinter of wood. At least not that anyone could tell. Everyone followed Nikita's orders. The brothers that owned the company were more than pleased about how things had progressed under the watchful eyes, and sometimes hands, of their new supervisor. Nikita never thought that he'd like it here, but the job, the room at the Landing, and the newfound respect that he received made him think that he'd stay here a little longer than he had first thought.

23

If one would mix a late night of gambling with a lot of whiskey and cigars, then sprinkle an early bright sunlight coming through Nikita's window, then one could understand why the short-tempered Nikita was so intolerable. Even the red-haired woman knew it was gonna be bad. She anticipated the rooster's crow and skipped out of Nikita's room just in the nick of time. His head was pounding from the massive indulgence from last night. He sat on the edge of his bed cursing himself for losing control as he put his hand in his pocket and found most of his money was gone. *Did I lose all my money?* He thought. *Maybe somebody steal eet ven I pass out. It vas dat red-haired voman!* He always thought it was someone else's fault . . . never his. Even as he thought all of this, deep down he knew he gambled it all away.

He was mad.

He was furious.

He was agitated.

He staggered over to the wash basin. Instead of sticking his hands in it to bring water to his face, he submerged his whole face into that basin full of water. He blew his breath into the water making the water bubbly. He then pulled his wet face and soaked beard out of the water and shook his head like a wet dog. He used his shirt sleeve as a towel. Once his face was dry, he threw the wash basin across the room crashing into the far wall. He put on his Stetson and went in search of coffee.

He found his coffee. It was bitter, like his stomach and attitude, but it'll do for the time being. He overheard a couple of men at one of the tables talking about a man being caught cheating at poker. The man had been beaten silly. Nikita looked down at his knuckles. They weren't bloody nor swollen. He smiled at the thought of someone else being the muscle last night. For the last month or so, he had made a habit to drink his coffee as he gazed out through the wall size window on the landing. It was interesting for him to see the town grow using wood, brick, and stone. The season would be changing soon, and the backdrop of green trees would give way to leaves of red, yellow, brown, and orange.

He was halfway through his coffee as he watched some of the local business owners get their day started. There were a couple guys shoveling coal that had spilled off the top of one of the hopper cars away from the train tracks. Way on down the road, Nikita could see the barber sweeping the boardwalk in front of his shop. There was a minister in front of his church talking to an old man and young woman. They seemed to have brought the minister milk bottles. *De man must be de milkman and have hee's daughter wid heem,* thought Nikita. He kept watching them. He hadn't really noticed them since he was in town. As they got onto their milk wagon and made their way towards the landing, Nikita kept watching them. *Odd . . . there was something odd about that girl.* Thought Nikita. It was as if he knew her. He chuckled at the idea. He had only met a few people since he'd been here for the last month or so and one of them was definitely not a teenage girl.

But he kept an eye on them, a rather bloodshot eye that is. He watched them as they came to the landing and livery. They tied their horse and wagon to a hitching post out back at the livery stable. Nikita lost track of them. He turned away from the window and looked down into the saloon and dining area. He squatted down under the handrail to get a better view and almost fell backwards. *Blasted hangover,* he thought. He regained his composure as he used one hand to grip the rail.

There they were. The old man was talking to Mr. Losure as the girl carried in a second round of milk jars. She had delivered two milk carriers in each of her hands at once. She carried out the used empty milk jars in wooden milk carriers and then returned with what looked like a large container of butter. Nikita just stared. *I know dat girl. But how can eet be? Vere do I know her from?* Then suddenly it hit him. It hit him hard. The thought just about knocked him over. Francis Byrnes' daughter. The memories of him being cheated by Francis and of Elizabeth watching him kill her mom started to come back. The memories were just a couple steps ahead of the anger and hate but the latter was quickly catching up to the memories.

As he stood up, he dropped his coffee, spilling the half-filled cup on a couple of men as they ate breakfast on the main floor. Nikita brushed off the cursing and expletives coming from the men under him. He noticed her, the dairy farmer, and Mr. Losure looking towards the commotion that the men were creating. He ducked back away from being seen by Elizabeth. He had pressed himself against the large window so as to be out of their view. Part of Nikita wanted to rush down the stairs after the girl. The other part told him to lay low for a while to think things through before he left for work. As he made it to his room and closed the door, he knew darn well he wasn't going to work today.

The last few months had been great for Elizabeth. She worked long hard hours on the farm and that was okay with her. It kept her mind busy on the tasks at hand. Every day she became more and more confident with her job. It made her a more confident young woman. She still had a slight swagger to her step that was there to cover up her insecurities and trauma. Robert had noticed the confidence in Elizabeth grow day by day. He gave her more duties every week and she handled them all with ease. He even let her take on some tasks and responsibilities at the future dairy farm.

But Robert noticed one thing that Elizabeth did have to work on - her relations with customers. She could be a little impatient if a customer had questions about a delivery or wanted to change an order. Overall, he was glad to have her on the milk route with him and also on the farm. Ellen loved having her around just as much as he did, if not more. Ellen enjoyed having a female around. She treated her as her own, even though Elizabeth wasn't a girl that was into dresses and ribbons. She would rather pull a horse and wagon before she would ever think of playing with dolls and that was just fine.

Elizabeth loved being at the Wymer farm. She also had a growing fondness of the future dairy farm on the other side of Harrisburg. All the daily chaos was at the Wymer farm. The future farm was a place of serenity and peacefulness. There was a lot of work to be done out there such as ground clearing of trees and brush. Robert and his cousin had already built a barn on the grounds and were using it as a storage place for equipment and extra hay for the cows. The hay loft was full of it. Piles and piles of it. Elizabeth liked to climb the ladder up to the loft and jump in the hay. She could practically lose herself up there in the hay. Then she loved climbing down from the loft and heading to the back side of the farm where there was a pond. She would jump in and cool herself.

Most times though, this was a place of work. Leadfoot enjoyed being out there with her. There was a lot of work to be done, but there was no timetable or deadline. All that Robert asked was for there to be improvement every day they were out there. What got done this year meant that there was going to be less work to be done next year. The goal for the farm was to be operational after the following year. That meant more ground clearing for a couple more barns and buildings, a farmhouse, a well and so much more. Leadfoot's real job was not that labor intensive as it was in the beginning, but it was demanding. He started out stacking bricks in wagons so they could be hauled to job sites around town. His knowledge of building construction and a good word from Robert into the right ears had put him on track to get off the grunt jobs.

"Oh, Leadfoot," Elizabeth exclaimed, "that's great news! If you get more experience then you could buy a house, if you decide to stay here." The thought of that was exciting to Elizabeth, but it was anxiety building for Leadfoot. This has already been the longest that he's stayed in one place in a long time.

It was still summer, although fall was in the air. Elizabeth knew that it wouldn't be long until fall took over and forced summer to retire. She sat beside Robert as he guided the horse and milk wagon along their usual route through Harrisburg after they had finished with the Jonesboro route. Ellen had made a beautiful necklace by using the old chain and added the hand carved cross that Elizabeth had received in Ohio. She was overjoyed by the gift from Ellen and she was excited to show the local minister when they dropped off his supply of milk. After they left the church, their next stop was to Mr. Losure's hotel and livery. Mr Losure was one of Elizabeth's favorite people. He had the best stories from days gone by. She had told him that he should write them down and share them with other people. *Someday,* he thought, *someday.* He would usually let her feed the horses, if time permitted, but not today. They had to get back to the farm due to a heifer giving birth to her first calf. As Robert talked business with Mr. Losure, Elizabeth brought in the milk jars.

"Don't forget the butter that I ordered, young lady," teased Mr. Losure. She gave him the stink eye and they both laughed. She then went out to the wagon to retrieve it and laughed again at herself as she thought about Mr. Losure's comment. A few short months ago, she would have been ready to have a war of words with him. She had come a long way with her attitude. She felt safe, loved, and like she had a purpose. Elizabeth really loved it here in Harrisburg and didn't see herself ever leaving.

She walked back in through the livery and there was a commotion going on in the dining area. "What's going on in there? It seems too early for wrangling going on?"

"Oh," explained Robert, "It sounds like those two guys got coffee spilled on them. Someone must've been up on the landing above them and carelessly upset his coffee." She looked up through the rails to the landing but couldn't see anyone.

"Well, I don't see anyone up there," she said. "Whoever did it must've skedaddled away. Probably a good thing they did. Those two guys are fighting mad and are looking to tan a hide or two." They left Mr. Losure to tend to the situation and they went to finish their route and to check on the heifer.

25

A lot of decisions had to be made. First things first. Nikita wasn't working that day or even the next. He found Mr. Losure and asked him to send a stable boy to the job site to tell them he wasn't showing up for the next day or so. He got himself another cup of coffee and stared out the landing window once again, but this time he was looking for someone specific. He didn't see her, so he went back to his room to think. The more he thought, the angrier he got. Nikita never had to deal with loose ends. He always finished what he started and covered his tracks. Once he left Boston, he hadn't given the Byrne family much thought until he saw Elizabeth. He thought that he could leave Harrisburg. Having Elizabeth out of sight would keep her out of his mind. But Nikita was no runner. He wasn't going to let a "girl" run him out of town. If she was here then maybe Francis was too. Oh, that thought excited Nikita. He sat up on the edge of his bed. He could get the money that was owed to him. Then he could deal with the two of them for good. A loose end tightened up. That gave him new life.

Nikita went down and found Mr. Losure removing bales of hay from a wagon. He tried to think of a way to find out about Elizabeth without sparking Mr. Losure's curiosity. "Dat old man dat brought milk today," Nikita started, "I tought I see heem in de barber shop. He es old to have young daughter, yah?"

Mr. Losure answered as he finished up stacking a few bales of hay in the livery, "Well, that's not his daughter. She's no relation as a matter of fact." Nikita helped Mr. Losure stack the last bale on top of three others in the nearest stable. "She came in town with another gent." *Perfect. De udder man must be Francis,* thought Nikita. He rubbed his face with both hands as if to ward off hangover pain behind his eyes, but really it was to hide a smile that was forming on his face. Mr. Losure continued, "She came to town with a hobo that goes by the name Leadfoot Frankie. He's a big horse of a guy, but not as big as you. He does construction and I think he stays in the hobo yard behind one of the factories down by the river." Mr. Losure noticed Nikita looking ill. "What's the matter? You okay? You look a little green around the gills."

"Uh, yes, yes, I am okay," lied Nikita. "Too much veesky and smoke last night. I go to lie down," he said as he left Mr. Losure. In reality, he did feel sick to his stomach, but it was from the information he just received. So, it looked like he had to deal with just Elizabeth. Sounds easy enough . . . But the hobo puts a twist on things.

* * *

There was no gambling, drinking, or smoking for Nikita that night. He stayed in his room alone. He had to make a plan. He just didn't know how to start one this time. Maybe a good night's sleep would help him come up with one. He woke up earlier than usual and laid in bed thinking. He thought that coffee should be made by now, so he went down and got a cup and went back to his favorite spot on the landing to watch for the milk wagon. After about three cups of bitter coffee, Nikita perked up when he saw the milk wagon slowly move from building to building. Eventually it made its way to the landing and livery and sure enough there were the old man and Elizabeth. Nikita stayed out of sight and waited for them to leave. Once they left, he went and got on the horse that his bosses had supplied him for work business.

It was easy to locate them. He decided to play it smart and stay at a safe distance. The last thing he wanted to do was to catch their interest. It was mind numbing following them on their milk route. After about an hour they made their way west. They went across the bridge and past the northern edge of the small town of Jonesboro. He followed them to a long dirt lane. Once he got there, he jumped off and tied his horse to a maple tree that was out of sight. The tree had plenty of shade and lush green grass for the horse to eat. He thought it would be best if he followed on foot.

After a few minutes of walking on the edge of the dirt lane, it opened to the Wymer Farm. Nikita stayed in the tree line as he checked out the area. It didn't look to be a busy place. After a while as he chewed on a dried up biscuit, He caught movement from one of the barns. It was Elizabeth. She had taken buckets and other equipment to the side of a barn to wash them in an old water trough. He grinned. What luck. She was only about fifty feet away. He could drop her with his stolen revolver from that distance. He pulled it out and quickly found her in the sights.

Then suddenly she looked right up at him. He froze stiff. He knew that she must've spotted him, but how? He wasn't making any noise at all. She stood there staring right at him. Then she suddenly turned and sprinted back towards the barn after she dropped the buckets. Nikita was so caught off guard that he didn't know exactly what to do. She must've spotted him and gone for help. He knew that he had lost the element of surprise. He decided to head back to fetch his horse and regroup. He was walking swiftly down the lane when he heard a horse and wagon coming. For a moment he didn't know which way it was coming from, so he jumped into some bushes that lined part of the lane. He stayed still and saw a horse and wagon fly past him heading towards the farm.

A frustrated Nikita went back to his horse. He untied it and thought for a moment. *Dere es no vay she saw me. No way at all. It no make sense. Someting going on.* He took the horse further into the woods and tied him to another tree where no one could stumble upon it or catch sight of it. He went back towards the farm and found a different hiding place at the edge of the woods. From the hiding spot he could see the entrance to the barns and the house. He was also close enough to hear the farmer, Elizabeth, and a big burly guy talking. He could only make out a few random words, but he distinctly heard Elizabeth call the burly man "Leadfoot." *That dee guy that came on dee horse and wagon,* thought Nikita. *Must be stinkin' hobo dat came to town vid girl.*

The farmer rolled up his sleeves as the other two kept talking. He said something about needing help and Elizabeth went into the barn with him. Leadfoot shied away from the barn and looked like he was about to get sick as he walked to the front porch of the house. A woman came out and offered him some lemonade and they sat and chatted for a little bit. Nikita was getting discouraged. There were too many people around here for him to get to the girl. Nikita thought that he would stay in the hiding spot for a little while longer to see if his small aptitude for patience could win any information for him. After a few moments it paid off and resulted in information he needed to execute his plan in dealing with Elizabeth once and for all.

* * *

Elizabeth and Robert rushed through the rest of their route to get back to the farm to check on the heifer that was close to birthing a calf. She jumped off the wagon just as Robert pulled it to a halt. She ran into the barn to see what activity was afoot. Robert walked in the barn after he tied the horses at the water trough. He stepped in and saw a worried look on Elizabeth's face.

"What's happening to the mother?" She asked.

Robert responded with deep concern. "She's having a difficult labor." He stepped past her and squatted down to the cow to see what was happening. The animal bellowed and grunted. "Yeah, we may have to go in and help this young girl. Have you ever helped deliver a calf before, Elizabeth?" He knew the answer, but he couldn't resist asking.

"We?"

Robert laughed, "Yeah, we. Eventually it'll be you. Living on the farm is not just milking cows and delivering the product. There's a dirty side that you have to know." He laughed some more as she wrinkled her nose. "Why don't you take those pails and wash them out back? I'll yell for you if I need you."

Elizabeth took the stack of pails and some other smaller equipment back behind the barn to a washing trough. As she was cleaning the pails, her mind started to wander. She wondered if she had given her mother a rough delivery. Maybe it was a rather easy one. She got to thinking about her mother. She missed her. She wondered if her mom would like it here. Not all of Elizabeth's days were bad with her mom. A lot of them were happy even though her mom wasn't all that affectionate.

The heifer bellowed loudly and then grunted like Elizabeth had never heard. It startled her out of her daze. She stood straight up and stared dumbstruck out into the trees. *Did Robert yell for me? I guess I wasn't paying attention. Maybe I need to go check.* Then she heard Robert yell her name. This time she knew for sure. She dropped the pails and bolted around the barn to see what was the matter. The heifer was really struggling now. You could see it in her eyes. Elizabeth wished she could go and hug the heifer for support. Robert was working with it, but whatever he was doing wasn't working. Ten minutes or so after dealing with the animal, Elizabeth followed Robert out to get another drink of water.

Robert was trying to decide what to do when Leadfoot came up the dirt lane on a wagon. Robert tipped his hat to him as he pulled up beside them and climbed out. "Dang," said Leadfoot as he crinkled up his nose. "This place stinks more of manure every time I stop by."

"That's the smell of money, my good man," said Robert.

"We have ourselves a problem heifer," Elizabeth moaned. "She's in a bad state of labor and I have to help Robert try to deliver the calf." Leadfoot gagged at the thought. She couldn't decide whether he was faking or if it was a real gag. She knew he had a weak stomach for such things.

Leadfoot batted at a couple of flies that buzzed around his head. "I'd rather be behind the eight ball with a dozen wet heads fighting over one tin roof than to mess with a laboring animal."

A confused Robert just stared at Leadfoot and then drifted his gaze to Elizabeth. "I heard him speak English, but I didn't understand one word of that."

Elizabeth grinned as she proudly began to interpret what Leadfoot had said. "That means he would rather be in a troublesome spot with twelve alcoholic hobos fighting for a drink that was on the house."

Robert thought for a moment and then mumbled, "Tin roof . . . drink on the house." He grinned and sighed about the creativity and then got serious. "Okay, Elizabeth, we gotta get back to the heifer. Let's go." Elizabeth looked at Leadfoot and shrugged as she turned and followed Robert into the barn.

Ellen had just come out onto the front porch carrying a tray of cookies and a pitcher of homemade lemonade and glasses. She looked around for the other two. Leadfoot told her that they went back into the barn to deal with the heifer. Ellen also turned up her nose. "Well, these cookies and lemonade aren't going away by themselves." Leadfoot and Ellen enjoyed each other's company and the refreshments.

Leadfoot reached for one last cookie and said, "One more for the road and then I must be heading out. I just stopped by to let Elizabeth know that I'll be gone for the next day or so. I have to ride into Marion and attend a meeting later on this afternoon. I've been asked to provide my input into a couple of building projects, thanks to Robert and his connections."

Ellen smiled. Robert and she had taken quite a liking to Leadfoot. At first, she didn't know what to think of him and the lifestyle that he lived. But after getting to know him, she realized he was a kind soul and was a hardworking and trustworthy man. "You can thank Robert all you want, Leadfoot, but he couldn't and wouldn't have done it if he didn't believe in you and your abilities." Leadfoot got up and thanked Ellen for the snack and kind words. "I'll let Elizabeth know that you left and won't be around for a while. I think Robert was going to have her do some work over at the new dairy farm later on this afternoon. He said something about her going there and bringing back a wagon full of hay while he tended to the cows here."

Leadfoot jumped up on the wagon and led the horse down the lane after he waved goodbye to Ellen. He reached the end of the lane and looked over to his right. *That's odd,* he thought as he noticed some weeds that were beaten down. *It looks like someone, or something made a path through the weeds to the woods. Oh well.* Leadfoot didn't give it much thought. If he had and possibly went to investigate, then maybe he could have prevented what was to come later on that afternoon.

"You should have seen her, Ellen, I looked up at her and you would have thought she'd seen a ghost," Robert laughed as he told Ellen the news as he was rolling up the sleeves of a new clean shirt. He ate a tomato sandwich before heading back to the barn to check on Elizabeth. "At first, she didn't want to get all messy, but she could tell that the heifer was struggling a lot. I had to raise my voice a little to get her attention, but she jumped in and helped hold the cow down as I got the calf out. I'm real proud of her, Ellen. She's gonna do well here on the farms." He finished his sandwich and went back to the barn to check on the new mother and the calf. He stepped in and saw that they were in the same stall as before and Elizabeth was sitting on the short wall. "How are they doing?" He startled her. She quickly wiped her eyes.

Sniff. "Oh . . . they're doing fine." Another sniff. "It's kinda gross to watch her clean her baby though." Robert walked closer to Elizabeth.

"Yeah, it is. It looks like they are doing fine," he added. "There's nothing stronger than the love between a mother and her child whether it's animals or humans." They both watched the cow and her calf for a minute in silence.

"I wonder if my mother had a painful delivery," Elizabeth spoke as a tear trickled down her face. She wiped it away as another one slid down to the tip of her nose daring her to wipe it away so another could follow the stream. "From what I know, her whole life seemed painful." Robert wiped the tear away with his index finger and as promised another tear followed the trail of the previous one.

"From what little that you told me about your life, it sounds like it was rough, but I'm sure your mother loved you even if she didn't express it. I'm sure she wasn't perfect, but it sounds like you had a place to stay and had food, though it may not have been much. Use those hard times from the past to influence your present and your future." They sat in silence for a moment or so before Robert spoke again. "I was going to have you spend the rest of the afternoon going to the new farm to bring back a load of hay. Why don't you stay here? Get something to eat and tidy up around here and I'll go instead."

"One thing my mom did give me was an example on how to be weak. I'm not weak and never intend to be." Elizabeth got up and rubbed her red swollen eyes. She wasn't going to let a sad moment change the mood for the whole day. Work still had to be done. "If you don't mind, I'd rather go get the load of hay. I think a little air will do me good." Robert was fine with that. He'd rather stay here and get some other stuff done. Maybe even sneak in a little nap. Elizabeth got up and walked to the house to see what Ellen had made to eat. She came back out with a sandwich and her bindle stick and got the horse and wagon ready to go. She started to pull past the barn when Robert yelled to her to be safe. No truer words had been said that day.

27

Nikita's eavesdropping told him that Elizabeth was going to be at the other dairy farm by herself and that filthy hobo was leaving the area for the rest of the day and then some. The little patience he possessed had earned him that great reward. He thought about sneaking from his hiding place, but he didn't. Now this loose end can be knotted off forever. He thought about waiting for her to leave the Wymer farm and overtaking her before she cleared the dirt lane. But he was concerned that someone else would show up. He thought about following her through town until they reached the new dairy farm since he didn't know exactly where it was located. He was concerned that he would be spotted so he decided to untie his horse quickly before she left and go to his favorite spot, the large window at Losure's Landing and Livery. He could see the whole town from there.

He stopped at the livery and told Mr. Losure to keep his horse at the ready, that he was staying for only a few moments and may need to quickly leave. He walked through the saloon and grabbed a bottle of whiskey out of the barkeeps' hand. He then went up to the window and stared hard down at everyone that passed on Main Street. There were a lot of people out and about at this time of day. He started to worry a bit about his plan. What if he didn't see her? What if he lost her in the crowded streets? After about an hour his worry became dread. He had missed her somehow. He was feeling the effects of the whisky, but there was no way he could have missed her on that wagon. Even if he missed her going to the new farm, surely, he would have seen her going back to the Wymer farm . . . unless there was another route to the farm. Oh, the thought of waiting for her to pass by as she took another way just about did him in. He thought about asking Mr. Losure where the new dairy farm was located, but he thought that would seem suspicious. All he could do was sit and wait. He had to wait, and he hated it. He could feel a buzzing emanating from his brain from the anxiety that he had about missing out on a chance with the girl.

There she was.

There she was.

There she was.

Just taking her sweet time. Sitting high on the wagon. Holding on to the reins and directing the horse through the town like some pompous wretched queen expecting everyone to move out of her way. Of course, she was just sitting on the wagon like any innocent human being, but that wasn't the way he saw it. He never saw the world like it really was. When he saw Elizabeth, he saw loose ends. He saw money that her dad stole from him. He saw her mother, whom he killed. And he was not sure if Elizabeth had pointed to him as the murderer. He saw undone work that could be finished with one swift hand. Nikita raced down the stairs, taking them two at a time, slammed past a couple of customers in the saloon, hustled through the livery, untied the horse, and was off to stalk his prey. He stayed a whole block behind her so he wouldn't be seen. Pretty soon they reached the northeastern edge of Harrisburg. The traffic became nonexistent, and he was concerned that she would notice him and wonder why someone was following her. He decided to stop and let her go farther. Surely the farm wasn't that far away. He stopped at a stream that they had just crossed so his horse could get a drink, and then he tied the horse to a tree. The dirt lane turned into a path that was beaten down by wagon wheel tracks through grass. After he tied his horse, walked up a slight rise in the path. The buzz of anticipation filled his body as he saw the farm. There were a lot of downed trees around the premises which would provide him all the cover he needed. He saw two newly built barns that he presumed held equipment and hay. There were three lean-tos that were filled with chopped wood. He kept looking around as he approached the farm to make sure that no unexpected guests snuck up around him. He reached a large wood pile and hid behind it. He snuck a peek around the pile to check out the rest of the property. He was confident that no one else was there. Nikita's mind was telling him to run from his cover and rush the area until he found the girl. Though he was an impulsive person, his instincts told him to wait for the right opportunity. But he couldn't wait for long. It wouldn't take her too long to fill the wagon with hay.

"Get out of here!" he heard her yell. He flinched as he stepped back behind the wood pile when he heard the words. He could feel his heart beating in his ears from anxiety and anticipation. He thought that he may have been seen, but as he looked back around the wood pile, he saw a family of raccoons scurry out from one of the barn.

She was in that one.

He knew it.

He felt it.

Es now or never, he thought. *Just minutes dis veel be over.* Nikita took a deep breath and let it out slowly. He quickly walked towards the barn with a purpose. He took out the gun he had taken from Yeager's friend, then abruptly put it back in his pocket. He then pulled from his side the filet knife that he'd taken from Yeager. He wasn't going to take a chance of her surviving a gunshot wound. He was going to cut her to pieces.

Elizabeth reached the farm and went straight to the barn that stored hay. She guided the horse to back the wagon into the barn. That way she wouldn't have to drag hay all the way out. She also liked to unhitch the horse from the wagon while she was loading it. She took him to a horse trough and let him drink for a while. She went back into the barn to load the hay. She really wanted to hustle and get back to the calf and see how it was doing. She couldn't remember if Robert wanted the loose hay or the bales, so she decided to take both.

She heaved up a few bales onto the wagon and pushed them to the front using her bindle stick to guide them in place. She moved the next bale and a family of raccoons darted from behind it. She screamed, "Get out of here" to them as they ran past her and out the door. "Man, I hope there's no more of those," she said to no one.

She climbed the ladder into the loft. That was where the loose hay was stored. She got up there and found the pitchfork that they normally used. She picked up a few piles of hay and dropped them down into the wagon. Suddenly she heard the horse snort loudly. She looked out through the cracks of the barn siding down to the water trough. The horse wasn't there.

That's odd, she thought. She tossed the pitchfork down towards the wagon and it stuck into a hay bale. She climbed down from the loft and went outside to the trough. She noticed that the rope that tied the horse to the post was cut and she could see her horse running down the path. She noticed there were a couple spots of blood on the ground. *This was done on purpose. But there's no one else around,* she thought as she looked for clues of a threat. She didn't see anything. She went back into the barn to get the pitchfork and her bindle stick. She went to the wagon and the pitchfork wasn't there.

"My devushka, are you looking for dis?" Nikita asked as he stepped from inside the barn door holding out the pitchfork.

Elizabeth didn't understand.

Elizabeth couldn't understand at all.

Elizabeth was completely confused.

And then it clicked. She just stood there. Her mind told her to run, but her legs wouldn't move. She wanted to scream, but her lungs wouldn't inhale. *Breathe, you need to breathe,* she told herself. She just stood there completely frozen. Too scared to move. She kept looking at the pitchfork in his hand. There's no way she could get it out of his grasp. He noticed her looking at it.

"Yah, I not let you have dis pitchfork," he said. The evil spilling out of his mouth with every word he spoke. "If you have it den it es bigger than me knife." Nikita pulled out the filet knife and pointed it at Elizabeth. She noticed that the point of the knife had blood on it. "Yah, yah you see de blood on knife. Horses move quickly when yah poke eem." That greasy smile stood out through his grimy beard. It reminded her again of all the pain he inflicted in Boston. "I tought I not see you again. I not look for you. I just tought dat you . . . poof, gone. I watched you get on train in Boston and tought 'such a pity for you to go.' We could had fun times."

"You killed my mother!" Elizabeth shouted. Her legs allowed her to move slowly away from him towards the wagon, and yet away from her only escape route out the barn door.

"Okay," he said nonchalantly, "if you say so, but dere vas many I keeled. It mean notting to me. Lucky for you dat you got on train. Oooh, it was sooooo close to fffttt," he said as he sliced the air in front of him with the filet knife. His excitement was turning into agitation when he noticed that she was beginning to move away from him. He had to finish this once and for all. "Your papa stole many money from me," a pumped up Nikita barked out. "Now I steal you life." He licked his lips. He flung the barn doors closed. They closed with a thud shutting out a lot of the light, though enough light came through the windows and between the barn siding. He then started after Elizabeth. She moved away from him even more, keeping the wagon between them. She saw her bindle stick leaning against some bales of hay. She ran to it and grabbed it and then instinctively ducked. Her ducking may had saved her life because she could feel the air move past her as the pitchfork hit the wall and then clanged to the ground. It would have hit her in the shoulder if she hadn't ducked. Nikita was moving in on her rapidly, haphazardly slashing the knife in front of him. She wanted to grab the pitchfork, but there wasn't time. She slid under the wagon and kept to the middle. Nikita grabbed the pitchfork. He bent down and looked under the wagon from the front, keeping the doors to his back. All Elizabeth could see of him was his sweaty dark hair and beard. His eyes were blood red where they should have been white. Nikita lunged the pitchfork under the wagon at Elizabeth, never letting go of the handle. Again, again, again, again, again and again. Each time the metal tines scraping the barn's dirt floor narrowly missing her. He moved to the right side of the wagon and stabbed at her again and again and again. Every stab was thrown harder and harder with more frustration and more determination.

Elizabeth could hear Nikita breathing heavily from all his exertion. She took the opportunity and scurried out from under the wagon and ran towards the door. If she could get it open, she could outrun him to town and get help. She reached the barn doors, but they only partially opened, not far enough for her to squeeze through. It took her a second to realize that there was a shovel stuck through the handles.

Then it happened. Nikita threw the pitchfork, and it got her. Right in the left triceps. It wasn't deep, but deep enough to keep her from scampering away. One tine got her as the other two tines stuck in the barn door. She didn't want to cry out and let Nikita know that he got her, but she couldn't help it. She wailed so loud that it echoed through the barn.

Nikita smiled. Smiled through his heavy pants as he sucked in as much of the dusty air as he could to fight exhaustion. He walked slowly towards her. She was panicking and on the edge of hysteria. She had to get away or she was done for. She grabbed the pitchfork handle and tried to pry it out of the door and her arm. Back and forth, back and forth, back and forth as quickly and she could until it gave a little. She tore her arm away, ripping a deep three-inch gash in her triceps. Adrenaline was pumping through her veins so much that she didn't feel much pain. She checked to see if she still had her bindle stick wrapped around her back and looked for a place to escape.

"No, no, no, no, no!" Nikita shouted as he saw her remove the pitchfork. He was coming from the far end of the wagon and gaining ground. She looked around again. The only place for her was up. Up to the hayloft. Five quick steps got her to the ladder, and she climbed like a hungry monkey racing for the last ripe banana. She stood up there listening to Nikita ramble on in Russian. She was pretty sure they were mostly curse words. She tried to pry the ladder away from the loft, but it wouldn't budge. It was securely fastened. She ran over to one of the windows and broke out all the glass and thought about jumping, but it was simply too high. If she jumped, she would break a leg. She saw a haystack up there. It was piled up in the corner and about the size of two full wagons. She didn't know what to do. Jump out the window or hide in the pile of hay.

Nikita heard the crash of broken glass and thought that maybe she jumped. He hoped that she had. There would be no way that she could have survived. He ran over to a ground floor window and shot three shots out at something he thought was her, but it wasn't. *She must still be in loft,* he thought. He was starting to lose his composure and he randomly shot his last three shots up through the hayloft floor. A frustrated Nikita went over and pried the pitchfork out of the barn door. He clumsily climbed the ladder as quickly as he could. He wasn't as nimble as Elizabeth. He stood still for a moment or two as he gathered his senses. He went over to the window and looked out of the broken glass. There was no evidence of her jumping out as far as he could tell. He looked around for other hiding places. There wasn't much up there besides hay. Piles and piles of hay. *Dere es no vay to hide een hay,* he thought. *Eet all over da place up here, but dere ees nowhere to hide . . . unless een dat big pile of hay in da corner. If I can't find her, I have to go down outside and start fire een da barn. Smoke her out.* Nikita was super stressed and exhausted. He didn't think it would be so hard to kill a young woman like this. He regained his composure and started stabbing the hay pile. Stab, stab, stab, stab. Very organized stabs. He started from the far left and meticulously worked his way through the pile. Every stab that came up empty, meant the odds were increased for the next stab to hit pay dirt. Every stab became harder and followed with a growl. Each stab's growl became louder and louder, to the point that they became maniacal screams. Closer, stab. Closer, stab. Closer, stab.

* * *

Each stab was getting closer to Elizabeth as they were coming from her right side. She was trapped. She had to think quickly. As she tried to think of a way out, the stabs got closer. Stab, stab, stab. Closer, closer, closer. Luckily, she placed herself in the far end of the pile of hay. Nikita would have to hit the whole pile before he got to her, but the stabs were coming quickly. She had an idea, but she was going to have only one chance at it and the timing had to be near perfect. She guessed that he was about fifteen feet away from her. She tried to calm herself down and to take control of the situation. Fourteen feet away. The stabbings were coming quicker, and the growls became frenzied howls. Thirteen feet away, twelve, eleven, ten.

Nikita's muscles ached with every thrust of the pitchfork, but he knew he was getting closer and closer. He was running out of hay to stab. For a moment he thought about dropping the pitchfork and bombarding the part of the haystack that he hadn't worked over. But he wanted to feel and hear the pitchfork slash into his target. He was sooooo close. He was about ten feet away from the end of the haystack. His lungs burning for oxygen as his howls and screams tore through his vocal cords. Stab, ten feet. Stab, nine feet. Stab, eight, seven, six, five… the mark was hit.

Nikita sneered a psychotic sneer as the mark was hit again, again, again and again. The fight was over. His muscles didn't ache anymore. He seemed numbed to his strained vocal cords. His lungs did burn for air, but they wouldn't get much air because of the five stabs that Elizabeth thrusted to them with the blade at the end of her bindle stick. She stepped out of the pile of hay. She was covered with it. She could barely see him standing there through all of the hay dust. Nikita just stood there in awe. He wanted to bull rush her, but he didn't have the energy. He barely had the stamina to stay upright. He dropped the pitchfork and slowly reached for the filet knife, but he never got it out of its sheath. Elizabeth stuck him one more time in the chest and pushed hard this time. She pushed so hard that Nikita took two steps backward and lost his balance, fell from the loft and landed in the middle of the wagon full of hay. Elizabeth looked over the edge of the loft through the dusty air at Nikita laying there motionless as the hay soaked up the blood that was leaving his wounds. After about fifteen minutes of watching him, she laid on the edge of the loft and cried until Robert and Leadfoot came later that night to see what was taking her so long to get back.

29

Ellen had prepared a beautiful Sunday dinner. It was an annual thing the Wymers did to celebrate the first day of spring with a few friends from Harrisburg and Jonesboro. Hopefully the days coming would make them forget the cold winter. Winter days were always harder when one lived on a farm. But Elizabeth had welcomed the cold winter days. Those days were easier than the days just after the attack from Nikita.

After the meal was finished and everything was cleaned up, the women stayed in the kitchen and the men went out on the porch to smoke cigars and pipes. Elizabeth went out to the barn to check on the calf that was born late that past summer. The calf had grown bigger and was well on its way. There were two other heifers that would have their babies later in the spring. *Man, we'll be hitting it hard on the new farm this summer. We're going to run out of room here in no time,* Elizabeth thought. She heard a wagon pull up the dirt lane as the wheels sloshed through mud puddles. She went to the front of the barn to see Leadfoot guide the wagon to a stop at the barn's entrance.

Leadfoot received a big hug and smile from Elizabeth after he jumped off the wagon. "You just missed a delightful Ellen-cooked meal," she stated. "I bet if you go in the kitchen and give her that hobo-sad-puppy-dog-look that she would heat up a plate for you." Leadfoot proceeded to show off a sad signature look that he had used a time or two in the past. "Yep, that one will do fine. You wear it well."

Leadfoot went to the porch with the guys as Elizabeth went and told Ellen that he was there. She soon presented Leadfoot with a plate of warm-ups. Not wanting to be rude and eat in front of the others, he and Elizabeth went and sat in the barn.

He finished eating and looked around as they leaned against one of the farm's wagons. "Hey," he reminisced, "isn't this the same barn that we stayed in when we first got here?"

A peaceful Elizabeth smiled as she nodded her head yes. "Seems like a lifetime ago, but it hasn't even been a year."

"That's very true," he added, "but you've seen and have done more in the last year than most people see or do in a lifetime." Elizabeth smiled as she thought of the people that she met during the time on the rail. Some bad, but mostly good people. As she was fumbling with her wooden cross pendant, she noticed that Leadfoot acted like something was on his mind.

"You've had an adventurous year, also," she said. "Maybe not as venturesome as other years, but at least you got to meet me," she teased as she poked him in the ribs.

A tentative Leadfoot was hesitant about what he was going to say. "You love this place, Elizabeth, and it loves you back. This place needs you just as you need it. I'm glad you found the stability that you wanted and needed."

Elizabeth took a step back from Leadfoot. She didn't like how this conversation was going. She spoke with trepidation in her voice. "And you like it here in Harrisburg, too, right?" Angst filled her throat as she tried to choke it down when she saw Leadfoot slowly drop his chin to his chest. "Leadfoot, you're doing remarkable things here. Your new job has given you enough money to move into the Landing and out of that camp."

"Yeah, thanks to you for your help in creating an open room," joked Leadfoot in reference to Nikita's room becoming available.

Elizabeth said "You're welcome," with an exaggerated salute from her right eyebrow.

"Leadfoot, don't you like it here? You're making headway. Your life has meaning now. People like and respect you."

"Yes, my life has meaning," said Leadfoot. "Elizabeth, I love my life, I love this town, and I especially love the person you're becoming." They both went over and sat on the back of a wagon that was just inside the barn door. "Listen, when I'm here working, I am so thankful for the opportunity. I lay down each night and thank God Almighty for the circumstances that He has provided me. But I also thanked Him every night for the freedom and liberty to be able to move from place to place. Lately, I've been wondering what is going on in the big country. There's so much for me to see, Elizabeth."

Elizabeth was fretting. She didn't know what to say. "Leadfoot, I don't think I could leave this place. I consider you family. I consider the Wymer's family, too."

"And they are your family just as much as you and I are family. I'm not asking you to go with me. I'm telling you to stay. You don't need my help or protection now. I think that you've proven that quite well. But I need to go. I need to move. I need to keep moving. This is the longest I've stayed in one place since I started riding the rails. I'm way overdue to catch a ride on a steam hog."

Elizabeth was dejected but she understood. She was going to miss him with all her heart. Fighting back tears was a task that she was losing, she leaned over and gave him as huge a hug as she could muster. He wiped her tears away with his thumb. "So, when do you think you'll be leaving?"

"I've already left." Elizabeth was taken aback and had a confused look on her face as he explained, "I've already checked out of the Landing and already told my boss of my intentions. Now I've talked to you and I'm ready to go."

"Where are you going to go?"

"Come on, Tumbleweed, you know how this works," he joked.

"So, you're just going to start padding the hooves until the hooves stop, huh?" She joked. She knew the answer. Heck, she lived the answer. Elizabeth scooted off the wagon. "I want to walk with you for a while and say goodbye."

Leadfoot shook his head. "Not such a good idea there, Tumbleweed. Prolonging the inevitable will only make things worse. As far as it's concerned, we already said our goodbye's. You know this doesn't mean I'll never be back. I promise to always stop in whenever I'm back in this area. You can count on that."

And with that, Leadfoot jumped off the wagon and brushed off his pants. Elizabeth jumped off, too, and he hugged her once more and pointed his toes down the lane and headed towards the train track just outside of Harrisburg. There was no boxcars in sight when he got near the railroad. So, with a big smile on his face and his bindle stick on his shoulder, Leadfoot walked down the road to follow the rail curving alongside the river and headed east to the next adventure.

Leadfoot had just left Harrisburg and was enjoying the sun and the birds chirping as he walked along the train track when he heard the sound of horse galloping from behind him. Instinctively, he got off of the path and scurried down to a tree line out of sight. The horse and it's rider slowed down to where Leadfoot was in the trees.

"I saw you go in there, Leadfoot," teased Elizabeth as she was getting off of her horse. I have a favor to ask of you."

Leadfoot stepped out of the trees and teasingly said, "You've become an excellent tracker to find me. What is the favor, Tumbleweed? I thought we already said our goodbyes."

She pulled out a meat cleaver. "This is the cleaver that Papa Gio loaned me. He told me that I could have it until I didn't need it anymore. I think the day of me not needing it is here." She reached out to give it to him, but he was hesitant at first. He eventually took it.

"I remember that day," Leadfoot said as he looked over it. "You're right on what he said, but I bet he would like to see you bring it to him.

Elizabeth was somewhat taken aback. "But, I'm staying here. I'm done riding the rails. I plan to never go back."

"Never is a long time, Elizabeth. Are you sure?"

Elizabeth was sure.

Elizabeth was never more sure.

Elizabeth would never be more sure.

CPSIA information can be obtained
at www.ICGtesting.com
Printed in the USA
LVHW041533120623
749513LV00006B/637